POLAROIDS

by

Jim Butler

IBEX
New York

Printed in the United States of America
ISBN-13: 978-0615846439

“You can count on one thing, that the reason they call it fiction is it *is* fiction—that any writer is a congenital liar incapable of telling the truth, and so even he can never say how much he embroidered, imagined anything because he simply could not take any fact he saw and let it alone. He’s convinced he can do much better than God could, so he’s going to improve it—change it.”

William Faulkner, West Point, 1962

For Nell, first reader and permanent love

and

Sonia Pilcer and Beth Bauman, two exceptional writers who provided inspiration and guidance through every story in this collection,

The Writer's Voice, for establishing the program that allowed me to meet Sonia, Beth, and all the others,

and Jeff and Louise Kindley, who caused this book to happen.

"The Grand Inquisitor Comes to Tennessee" appeared first in *SundaySalon.com* August, 2008

"Sugar Pie" appeared first in *Steel Toe Review.com* October, 2011

Table of Contents

New York, 1966

Polaroids

The basement of McGovern's Tavern on Columbus Avenue in New York was dark and damp and, today, disappointing. No—worse than disappointing. Disastrous. The Cassie Sullivan Polaroids had to be here—but they weren't.

When Jackie Barron had moved back to Los Angeles from New York a year earlier he knew it was temporary, so he stopped by McGovern's to ask for some empty beer cartons to use for storage.

Paddy McGovern, the neighborhood saloonkeeper who had become his friend and advisor, had been outraged at the idea.

"God knows I've an abundance of beer cartons," he said, "but you'll not pay those crooks at some warehouse for storage when I've got a basement with enough empty space to park a car. Leave whatever you want to here with me; every thief in the neighborhood thinks I'm watched over by the Irish Mafia. This place is as safe as the Vatican. Safer; there's some of those priests in Rome I wouldn't trust with a nickel's worth of chocolate. "

Jackie didn't own anything that was worth much more than a nickel's worth of chocolate, so he was delighted by the offer.

That was then. Now it was six months into 1966 and Jackie was back, as expected. What he hadn't expected was that he'd be living temporarily with Cassie. Their affair had been pretty near perfect except when it wasn't, but when he left for California they weren't speaking. Then, while he was in L.A., she came to town on business, he visited her at her hotel, he stayed the night, and they were speaking once again. Except when their mouths were full of each other.

Given this revived intimacy, it seemed only natural that he should move in with her while he looked for an apartment. He never quite understood why they kept breaking up in the first place—Cassandra Sullivan was without challenge the most thrilling woman he had ever known—the only thrilling woman he'd ever known intimately—and that was only partially for shallow reasons.

He wondered how long it would last this time.

The trouble—the trouble that had him crawling around on the concrete floor of McGovern's Tavern—had begun the night before. Jackie had a new camera and he was pleading to take new pictures of Cassie.

"Okay," she finally said, when he described the tastefully provocative photos he had in mind, "but where are those naked Polaroids you talked me into last year? The ones nobody in the entire history of the world was ever going to see?"

"As, indeed, no one has," he said immediately. "And technically you weren't really naked. You were wearing stockings and high heels. Anyway, they're safe in a box in Paddy McGovern's cellar."

"How safe?" she said. "Tell me you bought a steel box with an unbreakable lock."

"Don't worry about it, beauty. They're not exactly in a steel box, but they're not in danger of pilferage by some horny teenager. Nobody's going to pilfer you but me."

Cassandra Sullivan was not amused. “I’d had too much to drink that night, Jackie—”

“Yeah; me too,” he said.

“You’ve always had too much to drink; that’s not the point. The point is, I don’t remember every picture, but there were some that were fun when I was drunk and worry me a lot now.”

“I’ll pick up all my stuff as soon as I’ve found a place, and I’ll bring the Polaroids directly here. I promise. We can have a terrific evening just recreating those shots. Although I’m thirty-one now; I may be too old for some of them. Anyway, you can come with me and—”

“No, I cannot come with you, Jackie! You think I’m going to stand there while you’re digging around for nasty pictures starring me? You go! And don’t discuss it with Paddy.”

Which was why, the following afternoon, Jackie Barron was in a state of despair. He had gone through everything. The box with his winter socks and shirts, the larger box with the three-speed phonograph Cassie had given him for Christmas the year they met. Another box with LPs by Charlie Parker and Chet Baker and Frank Sinatra. A larger one with every letter he had received since 1955. Books stacked high in cartons. A folder with pictures of his friends and several—perfectly decent—snapshots of Cassie in Riverside Park. Everything he remembered leaving behind was here.

Except a shoebox with a dozen Polaroids.

It wasn’t only the potential wrath of Cassandra that was driving him into a frenzy. Even more than that was the loss of pictures that pretty much satisfied every fantasy he'd ever had and some he hadn't dared to have. Pictures so dear to him that he was afraid to carry them across country lest something should happen to them.

Now something had happened. And what were the odds that Cassie would say, "Oh, that's all right; we'll just do it all over again"? He should live so long.

"What in the name of God are ye scrabbling around for, Sean?" Paddy McGovern, who was coming carefully down the stairs, sometimes called Jackie "Sean".

"There's something I can't find, Paddy," he said. "It's just an old shoebox, but it's important. Believe me, it's *important.*"

"Ah," the saloonkeeper said. "The shoebox. I was meaning to tell you about that."

"What? What, Paddy?"

"Well... we had a little flood down here when that pipe behind you broke. Nothing terrible; you'll find most all of your things don't even show a mark. But that shoebox was in a carton right under it, and the water soaked through, and... it soaked through the shoebox a little."

"Oh," Jackie said.

"That's the bad news. The good news is: no damage done. I'm sure you'll find the contents weren't harmed."

"What... uh... what *happened* to the *contents*, Patrick?"

"Not to worry, lad, they're fine. You can't find them because there were a lot of workers mucking around down here so I locked them up in my office. Didn't I promise you everything would be safe?"

Jackie took a very deep breath and exhaled slowly. "I don't know if you looked at what was in there," he said, "but... uh..."

"Jackie, did you ever know me to stick my nose in where it doesn't belong? Just relax. Come on back up with me and I'll get your package out of the safe."

"Thank you. *Thank* you, Paddy. Cassie was worried that... well, she was just worried."

"I know; she always worries that she looks fat just because she has those abundant bosoms."

Patrick McGovern was a man who could actually chuckle, and he did. "Well... tell her she doesn't look fat."

He was slowly climbing back up the stairs.

"Just don't tell her it was me as said it."

Hutchins, Tennessee, 1947

The Grand Inquisitor Comes to Tennessee

Even while he was attacking his friend Walter Bob Feston, practically accusing him of being possessed by the Devil, Jackie Barron knew that he was out of control, sounding like a revival preacher he once heard, calling down hellfire and damnation. It was not like him.

Jackie went to church, of course. Going to church and loving Jesus was taken for granted in Cherokee, Tennessee; it was like eating supper, or loving your mother. Being a good person just naturally meant going to Sunday School in the church basement at nine o'clock on Sunday morning, then going upstairs for the sermon at ten o'clock, and—this was mostly women—going to Prayer Meeting on Wednesday night.

Jackie did all that, but he sure never went around talking about God and Jesus all the time—or any of the time.

He didn't have a clear picture of Heaven—angels and harps and clouds didn't really sound like all that much fun—but he had a clear picture of Hell in his mind. Brother Jennings preached about Hell a lot, and the way he described it—just as clear as if he'd been there—it was all horrible fires that burned your feet, and having sores all over your face, and everybody screaming "I'm sorry!" after it was already too late. Jackie knew he would do pretty near anything not to go there.

Still, that didn't really explain why Jesus and the Devil and everything just seemed to take him over that day at Walter Bob's house. He'd gone there to trade comic books, the way he always did. He had read his new Captain Marvel and Submariner and The Torch enough times, and he knew Walter Bob would have the new Superman, and Plastic Man, and Wonder Woman—who was darn good for a girl, although Jackie wouldn't ever want anybody to see him buying one.

When they finished, Walter Bob didn't want Jackie to leave. Jackie knew that was because Walter Bob didn't have too many friends—maybe not any others. He was funny-looking and he was the only kid in sixth grade—maybe the only kid in town—who wore glasses, and the other kids made fun of him.

Jackie thought he was okay, and sometimes they played checkers together. The truth was, Jackie kinda liked being somebody's only friend, and he liked it that Walter Bob looked up to him—the way Jackie looked up to Eddie Garrett, who was popular and tough and already doing stuff with girls.

"Wait a minute," Walter Bob said. "Don't go yet. I heard a real good joke from my cousin and I'll tell it to you. You want to hear it?"

"Okay," Jackie said. " Go ahead."

Walter Bob, very excited, snickered through his nose and said, "It's really a riddle, and this is what it is: What was the last thing Jesus said on the cross?"

"I don't know. What?"

"He said 'Jesus *Christ* that stings!'"

Walter Bob laughed his laugh that sounded like hiccupping. Jackie didn't laugh. He knew you weren't supposed to make jokes about Jesus. Walter Bob knew it too, because he took one look at the darkness on Jackie's face and stopped laughing.

"Walter Bob... how could you tell that? You made fun of Jesus!"

Jackie could tell by the look on his face that Walter Bob knew he was in trouble, but he was surprised by the panic in his friend's voice.

"I didn't think about it that way, Jackie. I'm sorry! I shouldn't of told that, and I never will again! You're not mad at me, are you? Don't be mad."

Jackie knew what it was like to be afraid of what grownups might say about something, but this was the first time anybody ever looked at *him* and looked scared.

It felt strange. It didn't feel bad.

"Will you tell your mother and Brother Jennings or do I have to?" he said. "If you don't tell—and I don't, either—it's the same as lying. I can't lie for you, Walter Bob. That's a sin, too. And I don't know if we can be friends any more. Maybe you should just take back your comic books and give me mine. You said a *joke* about Our Lord Jesus Christ!"

There were tears behind Walter Bob's thick glasses now. He got up from the washtub he'd been sitting on and fell on his knees next to Jackie.

"*Please* don't be mad at me, Jackie! I'm sorry! I'll beg God to forgive me; I'll pray on my knees all night; I'll put all my allowance money and my lawn-mowing money in the church basket next Sunday. Please don't tell! I'll do whatever you think I ought to do. I'm ashamed of me, Jackie!"

Jackie Barron had never known a feeling like this before. Somebody was begging *him* for something. Somebody was on his knees to *him*. He could dispense mercy. Or not.

"Get on up, Walter Bob," he said finally. "If you beg Jesus to forgive you... and you read a chapter of the Bible every night... I know He will. He's merciful. I maybe can't be your friend for a while, but I won't tell anybody. And you can keep those comic books. You just need to be all clean with God before the next ones come out."

Walter Bob, his swallowed sobs jerking his chest in tiny spasms, took Jackie's hand and held it tightly. "I promise!" he said. "I hope I die if I ever say anything like that again. Just please don't stop being my friend. Please."

Jackie put his free hand on the other boy's shoulder and said, "He forgave the people who crucified Him; I know He'll forgive you. And I will, too."

Jackie took the comic books he had traded his for, and walked slowly home, thinking about what just happened. He was surprised because the more he thought, and remembered, the more he didn't feel good about it any more. Not at all.

New York, 1956

Skyrockets, Crashing Waves and a Train in the Tunnel

Even in the sexually constipated 50s it felt weird, unnatural, often painful and relentlessly terrifying to be a 21-year-old male virgin in Manhattan. It also seemed probable to Jackie Barron that it was a merciless but somehow well-deserved judgment handed down from on high. (It wasn't necessary to believe in God to believe in a mean-spirited deity.)

Still, as his boxers hit the floor he was praying ("to-whom-it-may-concern") that he was about to say goodbye to all that.

Beth Lerner had helped him through the frustrating process of unhooking her brassiere when his hands proved incapable of holding onto anything more intricate than her breast. At 19 she was a sophomore at Douglass College and she was as inexperienced as he was, but she seemed to welcome her deflowering with a sense of adventure. Not at all like Jackie's dread of another potential disaster.

Now she was lying on his bed in his apartment, all four-foot-eleven of her, as naked and as breathtaking in life as she was in his fantasies.

The bed was a mattress on the floor in a bedroom slightly larger than a storage closet, but Beth was there and he was there and the sheets were clean and this, it seemed at that moment, was absolute proof that there might be a God after all.

And then, as he dropped to the mattress beside her, she shattered that blissful epiphany by asking: "Do you have a... *thing*?"

Jackie's brain was already deprived of oxygen and blood—both had been rerouted to fuel the tumult below his waist—and her question threatened to leave him with no reason to continue living.

His eyes, already grown huge to make room for the vision before them, grew larger yet. His jaw dropped and his hand reached protectively for the erection that leaned against his belly.

"Of course I've got a *thing*," he said. "Is there something wrong? Am I too...? Is it...?"

He stopped talking, because Beth laughed. Beth could laugh in delight when she thought something was silly without ever making him feel she was laughing at him. That was one of the things he loved most about her. That and the fact that he had trouble looking at her and breathing at the same time. And that she made him feel tall when she stood next to him.

"I know you've got *that* thing," she said, pushing his hand away from the thing in question and replacing it with her own. "Seems like you always have *that* thing. I mean... a *thing*. You know. A *prophylactic*?" She shuddered. "God, I hate that word. It sounds like a wooden leg or something. But I hate *rubber* even worse. Don't you?"

Jackie found just enough breath available to mumble, "No. No, I didn't... I thought... I thought I could... you know... pull out. Before anything... happens. Is that all right?"

No one had ever mentioned the worthlessness of this particular birth-control myth to them, so Beth simply said, "I guess it's all right. Just be careful... okay? *Really* careful." She opened her arms to him.

Feeling her breasts against his bare chest for the first time he said, with innocent honesty, "I love you more than I ever loved anyone in my entire life!" He was aware that he had loved every girl he had ever loved more than he had ever loved anyone in his entire life, but there was no lie or exaggeration involved. He really had loved them all—all three of them—more than he had ever loved anyone in his entire life. It was always true, but with Beth it was even truer.

Jackie had been uncertain about bringing her to the cold-water flat where he lived. The toilet was in the hall, the bathtub was in the kitchen, one wall in the front room was painted black, the bedroom had a doorway but not a door, and the only heat would be whatever they generated on their own. He stopped feeling uncertain about this when he saw Beth's responses. She totally approved of this hovel as the appropriate home for a sensitive young poet, or actor or novelist or whatever it was that Jackie would eventually prove to be. The phonograph continuously playing Frank Sinatra or Chet Baker provided all the elegance they needed.

Jackie carefully, tenderly—he hoped—entered Beth Lerner. He knew as he did so that he would forever remember every detail of every tense, delirious, frightened, ecstatic, cautious, wild and free *instant* of these moments. And, God! he hoped they would last longer than moments.

It would be with a bitter-sweet sadness that he would realize, not so many years later, how few details he actually did remember.

He remembered his own amazement at the blood spot on the sheet afterwards. What he had read and the jokes he'd heard had caused him to expect a veritable hemorrhage of blood, soaking the bed. The actuality was about the size of a quarter. The blood spot didn't wash out, so he saved the sheet and slept on it to feel close to her.

He would remember that he withdrew from her body, then and always thereafter, as promised. He would remember her telling him a few months later that she might be pregnant anyway. He would remember the later, joyful phone call when she found she wasn't.

He continued wrapping himself in the sheet until the following summer, when Beth turned twenty and transferred to Antioch College in Ohio and told him she was also sleeping with the fellow student who drove her home at the end of the term.

Jackie threw away the sheet. He did not throw away the pictures he had made of her, although he did hide them whenever he met a girl he loved more than he had ever loved anyone in his entire life. But that didn't happen again for many weeks.

Hutchins, Tennessee, 1945

Sugar Pie

When Jackie Barron was doing something real bad—like running in the house or talking back to his grandmother—she would grab aholt of his arm and say, "Boy, if you keep actin' out your Uncle Isaac is going to come and get you and put you in the pokey!"

Jackie's uncle was the sheriff in Hutchins County, Tennessee, and Jackie stayed a little while with Uncle Isaac and Aunt Norrie every summer. They lived right there on the first floor of the jailhouse in Coal Creek. You had to walk up a real steep staircase to get to the lockup, which was on the second floor, and Jackie liked to play up there in the cells, which were usually empty.

The summer when he was ten years old was the summer when he met the prisoner whose name was Alonzo.

Aunt Norrie had picked Jackie up in their '41 Ford—they had an old Packard station wagon that Uncle Isaac used when he was doing sheriff work—and they talked about all kind of things on the drive back to Coal Creek. Jackie always liked talking to Aunt Norrie because she was interested in just about everything that there was, and she talked to him just like he was a grownup.

When they pulled up at the jailhouse, Uncle Isaac—looking to Jackie like he was ten feet tall—was headed for the backyard carrying one of them great big pots that he'd probably took off a moonshiner when he busted up his still. One time Jackie heard his granddaddy talking to his buddy from the Mason's Lodge, and his granddaddy was saying, "You ever notice how Isaac don't never *arrest* the moonshiners? 'Course he don't. Before he got Jesus, he used to be one of their best customers. Isaac may be a lot of things, but he's not no damn hypocrite."

The sheriff stopped long enough to ruffle Jackie's hair and say, "You behave yourself and keep your Aunt Norrie company, boy. I'll see you at supper."

That was just about all Jackie would hear him say all summer. At first he used to worry that his uncle didn't like him, but Aunt Norrie said, "No, he loves you, Jackie; he's just not one for a lot of talking. He doesn't talk all that much to me, either. In the days when he was drinking you couldn't shut him up, but those days are gone. Sometimes I almost miss them."

After Jackie put his clothes and stuff in the room they always saved for him, he came back out to the living room, where Aunt Norrie already had the ice-tea and the checkerboard all set up.

While they were playing, Aunt Norrie said, "I've got a surprise for you—we've got us a prisoner who's been here over a month! He did something real bad up in Kentucky, and we've got to wait for some papers before we can send him back. His name is Alonzo."

"Can I go up and look at him?" Jackie said.

"You don't go 'look at him,' Jackie. He's not a caged animal. I'll take you up and introduce you as soon as we finish this game."

After hearing that, Jackie had trouble concentrating on checkers. (He won anyway.) He figured the man named Alonzo must be somebody really special; he didn't remember anybody ever staying there in the jail for more than one night. About the worst that ever happened in Hutchins County was when some of the soldiers back from the big war with Hitler and Hirohito would get in a fight at the beer joint out on the highway. Uncle Isaac would bring them in and throw them in a cell to sober up. The next morning he'd just holler at them and let them loose. Isaac thought they all ought to be treated like heroes, and he wasn't about to drag them up in front of no judge.

When Aunt Norrie took Jackie upstairs the prisoner was stretched out on the bunk in his cell, with his head propped up on a pillow that looked just like the pillows in Jackie's room. All the other cells were empty, with mattresses folded up on top of the bedsprings.

There was a bucket of soapy water with a mop in it just outside the prisoner's cell. The door was standing wide open.

"Alonzo, you ought to pull that cell door shut when you're in there, "Aunt Norrie said. "This *is* a jail; you know." They both laughed and Alonzo pulled the door to, so that he was looking at them through bars.

Jackie could see that the man wasn't young–he hadn't shaved, and his whiskers had enough white to show that he was forty if he was a day. He'd grabbed his blue denim work shirt and put it on, but Jackie had seen some wiry arms sticking out of his undershirt. He wasn't a big man like Uncle Isaac, but he looked like he could take care of himself in a fight.

Aunt Norrie said, "Alonzo, this is my nephew Jackie; he's about the smartest little boy you'll ever meet."

The man named Alonzo laughed and said, "I'm pleased to meet you; I ain't known a lot of smart people in my life."

When they were going back downstairs, Jackie whispered "What did he do?"

"You know I don't talk about that kind of thing, Jackie," his aunt said. "Every prisoner's innocent until the court says he's guilty. Let's just say, I don't hold with what he did, but love can make a body do some terrible things."

"Is it all right if I go back up there tomorrow?"

"I don't see why not," Aunt Norrie said. "He's not really a bad man in his heart."

The next day, Jackie woke up to the sound of a hammer. When he peeked outside he saw it was Alonzo, nailing some boards together on the back porch. He looked up at Jackie and said, "Somebody's gonna break their neck on these stairs," and went back to hammering.

After breakfast, Jackie went outside and found Alonzo mowing the yard in front of the jail. Aunt Norrie was around the side of the building, pulling some weeds out of her little garden. When Jackie bent down to help her, he whispered, "Is it safe for him to be out like this when Uncle Isaac isn't here? Aren't you afraid he'll escape?"

Norrie smiled a sad kind of smile and said, "I don't think he'd run away, no matter what. I think he's just tired of running."

When he'd finished with the grass, Alonzo put the lawnmower away and said, "How y'all doing over there with them weeds?" Aunt Norrie said they were doing fine but Alonzo came over and helped them anyway.

After supper that night Jackie went upstairs with a new book Aunt Norrie gave him, and settled down in one of the cells. Everything was quiet for a while, until Alonzo stuck his head in the cell door and said, “What you reading?”

Jackie told him, and Alonzo asked him if it was any good, and Jackie said he guessed so; he hadn’t but just started it, and they were both quiet for a minute. Finally Alonzo said, “I ain’t much with books. I got nothing against them, but I didn’t have a whole lot of schooling. I wasn’t but seventeen when I got married. I got lucky, though. My wife’s daddy was in the railroad union—that’s the best union they is, you know—and he got me a good job. And I was good at it.”

“Why did you quit?” Jackie said.

Alonzo snorted. “I didn’t have no choice,” he said. “After what I done, I just took off running. But them railroad years paid off—that's how come I always knew which trains I could hide on without getting caught.”

Jackie could tell that Alonzo was the kind who didn’t stop when he started talking, so he just listened.

“That worked fine until I made the mistake of being with a Hutchins County moonshiner when your uncle made a raid to shut him down. I always knowed white lightnin' was gonna get me in trouble someday. If I'd of just bought me a Co-Cola somewheres I'd still be out there on the road.

“The sheriff was about to turn both of us loose until he recognized me. My face is on one of them Wanted posters he’s got downstairs. After that he didn’t have no choice but to haul me in.”

Alonzo seemed to be in a real good talking mood, so Jackie worked up his courage and asked why he was a wanted man.

"Because of my wife," Alonzo said. "She was a good woman—beautiful woman. *Real* beautiful woman. Voice all soft and warm; put me in mind of Dale Evans. Her name was Nola Jean but I just always called her Sugar Pie. It was the right name for her. She was sweet as sugar. And she smelled like pies right when they come out of the oven."

"What made her want to put you in jail?"

"Well, it wasn't all her fault. It's just, I come home early one night after I'd been away for a week on the Louisville-Cincinnati run. Her and my friend Jim-Bob Ellis was right there in my bed together. When you get older you'll understand why I had to do what I done."

"What did you do?" Jackie asked.

"I kilt her," Alonzo said.

"Why'd you do that for?"

The old man just shrugged his shoulders, but his face got real sad.

"Wasn't nothing else I could do," he said. "I come from good church-going people and we don't believe in divorce."

Jackie was real quiet for a minute. Now Alonzo wasn't just a nice man he could talk to. Now he was like somebody in a picture show.

"Did you kill 'em both right there and then?"

Alonzo looked a little surprised.

"Naw," he said, "that wouldn't of been right. Like I told you, Sugar Pie was a fine, *fine*-lookin' woman. And if Jim-Bob had of been married to her and I wasn't? I reckon

I'd of done the same thing he done. So I didn't figger I had any right to kill *him*."

After that, Jackie spent a lot of time with Alonzo, helping out in the yard, and sometimes reading to him. Aunt Norrie brought up a kitchen chair for Jackie to sit on in Alonzo's cell.

The summer was almost at an end when the sheriff from Kentucky came to haul Alonzo away. Uncle Isaac and Aunt Norrie and Jackie were there to say goodbye, but they really didn't know what more they could say.

The Kentucky sheriff put Alonzo in handcuffs for the first time, and even slapped leg-irons on his ankles. "You don't have to do that," Uncle Isaac said, real quiet. "He ain't going to give you no trouble."

The Kentucky sheriff jerked on the chain, spit a little tobacco juice on the ground and said, "You damn right he ain't. He got away from me once and *nobody* gets away from me twice. That ain't the way we do things in Kentucky."

Jackie was sad to see Alonzo go, but he was glad he had met him and talked to him. He even understood why Alonzo had shot his wife but not the man who just couldn't resist her. Like Uncle Isaac, Alonzo didn't want to be no damn hypocrite.

Los Angeles, 1952

A Gentleman Is Born

"Don't worry about it," Art Lewis was saying. "My dad drives drunk most of the time and he's never gotten in trouble, so why should I? I'm a better driver than he'll ever be."

He spoke—slurred, really—with the unbridled confidence of a seventeen-year-old boy who, like most boys his age, thinks he's indestructible.

Art was the only one who had a car, so Jackie Barron and the two other friends who drove to the party with him had chipped in for gas and a couple dollars each for a bottle of vodka which Art's older brother bought for them. Nothing was too good for the almost-graduates of Lewis & Clark High, Class of '52.

The party was at Marv Glaser's house, and Marv had provided the potato chips and orange juice. The vodka was poured from inside the brown paper bag, just in case Marv's parents should change their minds and show up. Parents could be unreliable like that.

Buying their bottle—there were three others bottles at the party—had been a serious investment. A couple of dollars was almost a day's pay on Jackie's part-time after-school job, but he figured the money that bought his first drink just might be the most *interesting* money he'd ever spent. Or it just might be the worst mistake he'd ever made. He'd seen how one of his uncles behaved when he was drunk.

It seemed worth the gamble. Jackie felt he was 17 going on 30, and he was sure he would get drunk like

William Powell in the "Thin Man" movies; not like his Uncle Chris.

Getting drunk was going to be an important rite of passage; like the Indian kids they read about in history class. What the heck; Philip Marlowe drank all the time, and he never got sloppy. Jackie had seen Bogart and Dick Powell and Robert Montgomery all play Marlowe, and Bogart was best. He kept his bottle in the top right-hand drawer of his desk.

The fan magazines never came right out and said it, but he had heard that Bogart really drank like that off-screen. Alan Ladd, too. And Spencer Tracy. Jackie was willing to bet that none of them had waited until they were 21 so they could drink legally. Live fast, die young. The first part of that sounded so good that he figured it was worth taking a chance on the second part. Time to jump-start his real life, although he had decided to wait a while before he started smoking. One thing at a time.

"I'm not worried about you getting in trouble for driving shit-faced, Art," he said. "Trouble's good; it builds character. I'm worried about getting glass in my eyes when my head goes through the windshield. Okay?"

Jackie, Art Lewis and Tony Castenetti were standing together at the card tables that had been set up as the outdoor bar. Their other friend, Mark Beacon, was talking to a redhead and laughing a lot. Mark was always talking to one pretty girl or another; he didn't even need the drink.

A little earlier, Jackie had been talking to a pretty girl, too.

The plastic glass in his hand was filled with his third drink—or fourth, he wasn't sure exactly. Vodka and orange juice. Everybody knew that your parents couldn't smell vodka on your breath.

Truth was, by the time he had finished the first drink Jackie *wanted* people to smell it on his breath. Some of the kids were being very goody-goody and sticking to Coke and Pepsi; he wanted everybody to know he wasn't one of *those*. He was being one of the wild ones for the first time in his life, and it felt good.

The pretty girl was Marlene Egan, and Jackie had talked to her many times before. On all those times they had talked about her boyfriend troubles, or done homework together for English class. Marlene had no idea how insanely in love with her Jackie Barron was.

She'd been standing by herself. Her current boyfriend was Billy Gray, a hotshot football player who'd left her alone while he argued sports with two of the other jocks.

Jackie moved cautiously, doing nothing clumsy or over-eager when he joined her. He was wearing his own clothes, but he was wearing William Powell's eyes and Bogart's crooked smile. He didn't even *think* about trying to look like Alan Ladd; some things even vodka couldn't bring off.

Marlene was glad to see him. She was always glad to see him; Jackie knew that she liked him a lot. Just not *that* way.

He spoke softly to her until she said "I'm sorry, Jackie, I can't hear you over the music. What did you say?"

He told her again how beautiful she was tonight. He looked her directly in the eyes; something he had never done before. It felt weird, but it was worth it. She had great, dark eyes. He leaned over and spoke into her ear when he told her about her eyes. He did this cautiously—Jackie wasn't drunk enough to fight Billy Gray, even for Marlene Egan.

Somebody had put on a record by Billy Eckstein. He was singing *I Apologize*, but Jackie wasn't paying much attention to the words. It was a slow song; that's what mattered. With a slow song—particularly when it was after ten o'clock, like it was now—it wasn't just okay to dance real close to a girl. It's what you were supposed to do.

"I think it's time we had a dance together, don't you?" he said, pushing his voice as low as he could manage.

"I'm sorry—did you say 'dance'? I have a little trouble hearing you," she said.

He'd used the William Powell voice, which obviously wasn't working, so he raised the tone a little and tried Bogart.

Marlene smiled. "I'd love to," she said.

So they did. She had no objection to dancing close, even putting her head on his shoulder for a moment. He had always assumed he would die young, and this moment seemed as good a time as any. The odds of this moment ever happening in his life again were zero to none.

The music finished, and Marlene left her hand in his while they walked back to the spot where she'd been standing. Jackie looked around to see who was seeing this, and when he did he saw Billy Gray coming. Marlene noticed Jackie's attention wandering and followed his gaze, at which point she dropped his hand quickly.

He stayed to make small talk with Billy Gray for a moment. They didn't like each other, but Jackie didn't want Billy to think there had been something going on. Billy had a mean streak.

That's how Jackie wound up back at the card-table bar with his friends. None of the girls had shown any sign of wanting any one of them to stick around, and they were looking at watches. They were disappointed and they were ready to go home. Mark and the redhead were going to stick around for a while.

Jackie was ready to go, but he was not disappointed in the evening. He had experienced something wonderful. Something he could not imagine experiencing, so it must have been the drinks that did it. Girls really *liked* guys who drank.

Tony hadn't drunk much so he would do the driving. As they stumbled to the car—Art was the only one who fell—Jackie turned his head straight up as far as it would go, memorizing the stars.

That was a mistake. The electrical buzz in his head escalated to dizziness, the queasy feeling in his stomach worked its way up to his throat, and he knew he was in immediate danger of humiliating himself. He stopped, raised his hand like a crosswalk guard, and said "One moment. I have some business to take care of."

He fought the urge to run but still managed to get well away from the street lamp before stopping between two parked cars, carefully bracing himself with his hands on his knees, and vomiting—unseen—in the street.

It was over quickly. There was no way to rinse out his mouth, but he always carried Clorets chewing gum, since worrying about his breath was a constant.

He walked very slowly, very straight, maybe like Gary Cooper, although he wasn't sure if Cooper was much of a drinker. When he got back to his friends he waited until they were quiet before throwing his shoulders back and speaking.

"That," he said, "is how a *gentleman* gets sick!"

He liked saying that. He liked everything about the evening. The movies were right about the magic in a drink.

Maybe he didn't have to wait until next year to start smoking.

New York and points south, 1960

It's Always Foul Weather

The Great Blizzard of 1960 was already in progress when they left Manhattan, but it wasn't being called The Great Blizzard yet. It was a particularly nasty snow-storm, but in a New York March that wasn't headline news.

Jackie Barron was in the passenger seat. He had shaved on the morning of 9 March 60, which was the day he got out of the Army, which was exactly fifteen days and three hours earlier. He hadn't shaved since. And he might not ever shave again. Nobody could make him shave or cut his hair, because he was a civilian now so fuck off.

During the last storm like this he'd been in Basic Training at Fort Dix, where he spent two days shoveling the snow with something the Army called an "entrenching tool." It was a hand-held scoop, and under the circumstances it seemed to be the size of a soup spoon. And about that effective as a snow shovel.

He couldn't just get in a car and go away from that one. Now he could. After two years that felt like a prison term, he was ready to go anywhere with anyone. The fact that it would be warm in Miami Beach was just a happy coincidence.

Darby James was driving; the weary old '48 Buick was his. He'd been soldiering some damn where or other for thirteen years, and he usually managed to have some pitiful kind of car, even if he was stationed where it wasn't allowed.

This kind of independent thinking was why, after thirteen years as a Motor Pool driver, Darby was a Private for the fourth time. Every time he got promoted to Private First Class, or Corporal or even, once, buck Sergeant, he'd do something like insult an officer or throw up on a platoon sergeant or, like this last time, drive this car where he wasn't allowed to drive a car, and they would bust him down to Private again. He had been in the Army since he was eighteen years old and he kept re-enlisting.

"*Machs nix* to me," he'd say. (When he was stationed in Bremerhaven he'd learned to say *machs nix* instead of *I couldn't care less.*) "As long as I've got three squares and four walls I'm okay. Sergeant's got too much responsibility, anyway."

Darby was taking some leave time to go see his mother in Florida—he was a bad soldier but a good son—and a few days before Jackie got out, Darby asked him if he would like to come along for the ride. Jackie would. Jackie would have ridden with anybody to the far side of anywhere just to celebrate his freedom.

Now, headed for the West Side Drive, Darby said "We ought to hit Miami Beach in about 24 hours. Might take a little longer in this mess. My mother's place isn't air-conditioned and you'll be so hot you'll wish to God you were back in the snow."

Jackie doubted that, but either way it was okay. He was going someplace where he didn't salute anybody; where he could eat in a room that wasn't a mess hall. Driving to Miami Beach was such a fine idea that he wasn't worried about a little snow along the way or a little heat at the other end.

The further they got out of Manhattan the further away Florida seemed to be. An hour out of town they had covered about thirty miles, and the wiper blades were turning the windshield into a poorly erased blackboard.

"We might as well get out and walk," Jackie said. "I can just barely see the streetlights."

"You don't want to walk, because you *definitely* don't want to get out of the car," Darby said. "Last time I saw snow like this was Pusan in '53, and what you couldn't see there was North Koreans trying to kill you. So just enjoy the heater and relax; I'll get you where we're going."

Just south of Trenton they stopped off at a filling-station for gas, and Jackie was stunned to hear the guys who worked there saying things like *Y'uns ort not to be headin into this mess in this old crate,* and *Buddy, you need you some new tores on this thang; how fur you goin?*

It wasn't the advice that stunned Jackie; he had those fears himself. It was the accent. He knew it well—but he knew it from his childhood in the Smoky Mountains, not from a town just down the road a piece from Manhattan.

"Did you hear those guys?" he said as they pulled away.

"Get used to it," Darby said. "Here's a little trivia for you: about half of New Jersey is below the Mason-Dixon line. So, yeah. You're in redneck country from here on out. Ye-haw."

They drove in silence until Jackie said, "This seemed like a better idea when we were sitting in a warm barracks." They weren't passing through towns any more, and it was becoming harder to see by the minute. The moon was only an occasional visitor overhead, and roadside lights were mostly missing.

"Is this the best the heater can do?" he said. "I'm freezing my ass in here."

"Just stick with me, trooper; we'll get through this and—" Darby slammed his foot down on the brake as an animal, barely visible in the snowfall, raced across the road. The car's smooth tires found only a feeble grip on the icy surface and the car spun gracelessly around.

"Jesus Christ, Darby!"

"No sweat, GI," Darby said. "Everything's under control. I just like to spin the car occasionally; keeps me awake."

The motor had stalled but he was able to start it up again, and they continued ahead, moving very slowly on the treacherous pavement. Darby insisted on softly singing a country song about a plastic Jesus on the dashboard. He'd never had one, but he liked the song.

Hours crawled as slowly as the Buick did. Now they were on a country road with no lights at all; the snow hadn't ended but modern highways had. Their best guess was that they were in Virginia.

"We're gonna have to start getting out and scraping off the windshield," Darby said. "These wipers just aren't doing the job. You want to take the first shift?"

"I don't even want to *think* about it," Jackie said, but he forced the door open—a layer of ice had formed a seal along the edge—and got out. The scraper he'd found in the glove compartment wasn't up to the job, and he finally used his elbows and fingernails to finish clearing the driver's side.

"I hoped to God I'd never see an entrenching-tool again," he said when he got back into the car, "but right now I'd give a year of my life—or five years of yours—to have one of those oversized soup spoons for that ice."

"If you're wishing, don't waste it on an entrenching-tool—wish for a flame-thrower," Darby said. "That's what we used on the ice in Korea."

They had gone less than a mile when Darby turned his head to Jackie and said, "Do your wishing now. I'm gonna have to pull off the road; I can't see anything beyond the hood of the car. Maybe we'll get lucky and the tanks will come and rescue us. That happened to me one time in Korea"

Jackie had kept his eyes straight ahead—he always kept his eyes straight ahead in a car, even if he wasn't driving—so he was first to see the feeble light turning onto the road in front of them.

"You figure that's General Patton and the Tanks Corp up ahead?"

"Oh, better," Darby said. "Much, much better. Thank you, Jesus; we've got a snow plow! I don't care if he leads us into his own driveway, where he goes, I go."

Rolling at 10 miles per hour behind the plow, the weary old Buick stopped sliding on the freshly-scraped road. The wind still drove snow against the windshield with the ferocity of a fire hose, but their progress was steady for an hour or so before Darby said, "Oh, shit."

"Oh shit *what*, Darby? What does *oh shit* mean?"

"It means he's a local boy, and I think we just passed the county line. I think he really is headed for his own driveway, and we're screwed."

"Follow him, man, just follow him!"

"Get real, Jackie. He *is* going back to his garage. He's definitely not going to Miami Beach. It's all right. I think it's easing up—a little. We'll just keep heading south until we see Cuba."

"C'mon, man; you said you'd follow him anywhere!" Jackie said, feeling no need to be rational.

"That was hyperbole, Jackie; *hyperbole* for Chrissake!"

Jackie Barron was not happy—and it wasn't easing up—but there was no point in arguing. It was Darby's car, and Darby was the one who'd survived combat. Darby had a 100% record for saving his own ass.

They maintained an uneasy silence until somewhere in North Carolina. They had been listening to storm reports—nasty ones—on station WTRG in Rocky Mount when their radio finally gave up the battle and switched to all-static-all-the-time. Breaking the silence with oaths and pounding it didn't help, but Jackie kept trying until Darby reached out an arm to still him.

"Let it go, Jackie. Radio's the least of our troubles."

"What do you mean? *What*?"

"Look at the gas gauge. We're running on empty, partner."

"No-no," Jackie said. "Do not say that. We just have to get over this hill."

And the motor died.

Grinding the key didn't help. Pounding the dashboard in frustration didn't help. They now had the little engine that couldn't.

"Well," Darby said, "at least it's not the *worst* news we could get. I have worse news. We are now the frozen-food section of this meals-on-wheels. When the motor's not running, neither is the heater. If I perish first, save yourself. They say human flesh tastes just like raw chicken."

"Not gonna happen, "Jackie said. "Look up there. There's *light* on the other side of the hill! There's a damn *strong* light, and it's blinking. It's a summons. It's where we got to go. Up and over!"

Darby agreed. They climbed out of the car and ran uphill as best they could, each falling once on the slippery road. By the time they reached the top there were little ice-beads forming in Jackie's new beard.

Halfway down the other side of the hill was the source of the light—a neon sign blinking *GAS - EATS - GAS - EATS*.

"Okay," Darby shouted against the wind. "We gotta run for it. *Eats*, Jackie! *Eats* means stove; stove means heat. I'd run to China for eats and heat. Let's *go*!"

They went, staggering as gravity pushed them faster than they could run without falling. Jackie finally stumbled over his own feet. A rock hidden by the snow ripped a tear in the knee of the Army-issued khakis that he still wore.

They ran and they stumbled and they tried to protect their eyes with their hands as the wind-driven snow fought them every step of the way. And they made it, past the gas pumps and up the steps to the door of the diner, recognizing the woman behind the counter as their guardian angel.

But she was frowning.

She shook her head with annoyance, waving a dismissive hand at them. “You can’t come in here,” she said.

Jackie now understood what *nightmare* really meant. *Nightmare* was when you were shut out to die and you *weren’t* asleep.

“No... please...” he was saying, standing with Darby just inside the door. “We can’t... you’ve got to...”

The woman—Angel of Darkness now; not guardian—was trying to be heard over the wind that tore through the open door as she gestured repeatedly, pointing off to the other side of the diner. A large black man in an apron was walking through the room towards them, with his arms out, as if barring their way.

Darby was the first to figure it out.

“Oh, God,” he said, panting. “Un-fucking-believable. You know what she’s saying? You know what she’s saying, Jackie? She’s saying *Other side. Other side*! We’re in North Carolina, man! We’re in North Carolina and we’re on the *colored* side of the diner. We can’t come in here. We come in here, everybody goes to jail. We can’t come in!”

The man in the spattered apron had reached them. “I’m sorry, gentlemen,” he said. “You got to go around to the other door. We be happy to take care of you, but you got to go around to the other side of the diner. You understand?”

They understood. The two misplaced white boys from up north understood. They took deep breaths once more and ran around the side of the building and through the door; the white-people door.

The diner was built with the kitchen area running lengthways down the middle; separate dining rooms on either side. Two coffees were already waiting on the counter, and the waitress who hadn't welcomed them was there also. The smile on her face now *was* welcoming; amused but not scornful.

"I'mo bet you young gentlemens ain't from around here. Would I win that bet?"

"Yes, ma'am; we're sorry," Darby said, and she left them with menus. Jackie was silent for a long time.

"You hear about it," he finally said, more to himself than to Darby. "You hear about it, but you don't think about it happening to *you*. Standing in the doorway, thinking you're going to die, and you can't go *in*? All I could think was *Why me? What did I do?*"

Still shivering, he was spilling coffee over the rim of the cup. The cold was in the marrow of his bones. Maybe deeper.

"I know all about segregation," he said. "Everybody knows it's wrong. But Jesus H. Christ... *wrong's* too weak a word when it's about *you*, isn't it? When it's you it's about *burn-the-damn-place-down*; that's what it is."

He wasn't drinking the coffee. His hands were around it, absorbing the heat, but his head was down.

"I don't think I want to go to Florida," he said. "I just want to go home."

Darby shrugged. "I did two years at Fort Benning, Georgia. You never learn to like it, but you get used to it, Jackie. You get used to it. Down here it's always foul weather for somebody. This time it's us."

"Yeah," Jackie said. "Yeah. Lucky for us there's a White People side here. Otherwise we'd have to go someplace else only there isn't any place else so we'd just have to freeze and die, wouldn't we?"

He looked up. "Or else warm our hands over the ashes of the goddamn place."

New York, 1966

McGovern's Law

Jackie Barron had never felt uncomfortable being with women who were way out of his league. God knows they weren't hard to find. So far as he could tell, he had never known a woman who wasn't way out of his league. Which was okay. If it didn't bother them, he certainly wasn't going to let it bother him. Not that there had been all that many women in his life. Just more, he knew, than he deserved.

There was, however, one problem that Jackie had with all these exceptional women. Unlike his male friends, who stood a little in amazement if not awe at his capacity for hard drink, women who were involved with him all sooner or later decided that he drank too much. This perception was not in itself a surprise. After the age of about twenty—and he was in a whole new decade now—there hadn't been a time when he didn't think that himself. He just didn't see anything wrong with it.

He once, as a lark, let himself be talked into attending a traditional self-help meeting where someone insisted that, for those in the room, "one drink is too many and twenty are not enough." That sounded about right to Jackie. It meant that he was at least four drinks behind for the evening, so he left the meeting and went to McGovern's, the bar around the corner where he could start catching up.

The love-out-of-his-league who was back in his life at the moment was Cassandra Sullivan, and he knew there was a growing probability that she would not be back a whole lot longer.

His problem with Cassie was just a difference of opinion. The difference between her opinion of his drinking habits and his was that she thought he should do something about them. And she thought she could help.

She wasn't subtle in her efforts. Sometimes, after she'd stayed over, he would wake up and find her gone. When he finally stumbled out of bed he would push his feet into his slippers and find a scrap of paper tucked into the toe. Sometimes in both slippers. *647-1680* would be written on it. He knew what the number was. It wasn't her number.

In the bathroom he would find a note on the mirror saying something like "*You don't have to brush your teeth before you call AA. They won't care.*" At first he would laugh, and think it was a loving and caring thing to do. She obviously meant well. She'd learn to understand after a while.

She didn't learn to understand, and he learned not to laugh, nor to give a damn about how loving and caring it was. He didn't care how well she meant. It got old.

One evening she arrived unannounced and he knew from the expression on her face that something serious was coming. He hated that look; Jackie felt that everything in his life was already more serious than he could deal with, and he didn't need her to flash *SERIOUS SERIOUS SERIOUS* at him in neon.

He took a quick look around the apartment before going to the door. It wasn't in great shape but it wasn't bad. He wasn't exactly sure what he'd done the night before, but whatever it was, it hadn't been tidy.

He wasn't in great shape, either, but getting straightened out was not high on his list of priorities.

As soon as he opened the door Cassie looked at the drink in his hand and then she looked at the rest of him. Neither look looked happy.

Jackie didn't want to fight with her. Who'd want to fight with a girl this extraordinary? Her background was very Irish-American, with that white-on-white skin the Irish walk around in. Except that by her generation in America it had usually been destroyed on the beach. Hers was the smoothest and whitest white he'd ever seen outside of a porcelain vase. (Or a toilet bowl, but he never used that image when talking to her. She definitely had a sense of humor, but there were limits.)

It's true that he was a little obsessed with Cassandra Sullivan's looks, but he figured anybody who didn't obsess a little about Cassie's looks wasn't looking.

Women noticed, too. He loved it when he'd catch some other woman staring out of the corner of her eye, looking at Cassie's amazing bustline and hating her for it. Cassie's bustline was obviously real—women always knew that kind of stuff—and to some people this seemed to be unforgivably unfair. Nobody had the right to look like that without surgical assistance.

Still, he did not underestimate her just because she was beautiful. She not only wasn't dumb, she wasn't even blonde. She'd survived a miserable childhood, one she only referred to with clenched teeth. He wasn't unaware or unappreciative that she had come out of it gentle and intuitive. She consoled him when he hurt, then made him feel like he was the healer when life was emotionally stomping on *her*. And she honest-to-God didn't know just how extraordinary she was.

Jackie knew all that.

But there was one other trait that came with the wonder that was Cassie. She could also be a major pain in the ass, and this was clearly going to be a major-pain-in-the-ass night.

She got right to it: "We've got to talk, Jackie, because I can't keep on like this. And neither can you. You're thirty-one years old and you're not getting any younger. Keep going like this and you won't get any older, either."

Jackie turned his back to her and walked to his chair; she sat down very formally on the couch facing him. He didn't answer her rhetorical question and she didn't expect him to.

She said: "Have you called AA?"

He said, "Oh, I see. It's going to be one of those, is it?"

She said, "That means you haven't called."

He said: "No, I haven't called AA. And I haven't called Cardinal Spellman or Billy Graham. Or Mother Theresa. I do not need your help in this matter, Cassie. I do not need to find *647-1680* nailed to my forehead, which I'm sure is going to happen some morning."

His intention was to stay cool, making his point lightly and rationally, but he was maybe not doing exactly that. She most of all hated it when he got sarcastic, and he had an uneasy feeling that this was the road he was following. Not, he thought, that any of this was his fault.

All she had to do was say "*You're right, Jackie, I'm sorry,*" and that would be the end of it.

He was pretty sure she wasn't going to say that.

What she did say was, "Jackie, I know the thought of going through the rest of your life without a drink terrifies you. You—"

He interrupted. He hated to be rude, but sometimes interruptions were necessary.

"Going through the rest of my life without a drink is not an option, *Cassandra*," he said. He wasn't shouting or being sarcastic, but he knew that calling her *Cassandra* with that special *tone* usually meant he was on that path.

He said: "We're talking about more than a drink here, *Cassandra*. I'm not sure that going through the rest of my life without *anything* is an option."

He was rolling. "You're going to tell me you know that I can stop drinking if I really want to, and I'm going to tell you—three thousandth time, is it, or am I a couple times off?—three or four thousandth time, I'm going to tell you that you are absolutely right; I could quit if I wanted to.

"I don't want to, Cassandra. Of course I can quit. I'm like Mark Twain and smoking; I've quit many times. Proved my point and drank a toast to my will-power."

She was somehow not amused by his little joke—what can you do with a woman who doesn't find a reference to Mark Twain endearing?—so he turned up the heat.

"Have I ever hit you?" he said. "Have I ever lost a job? Been hospitalized? Been arrested? All right; I was arrested that one time, but that was in California and I only spent the one night in jail. If you've got to be a convict, the Beverly Hills Sheriff's office is a pretty upscale dungeon.

But if I'd known you were going to keep bringing it up like this I'd never have told you about it. Why do you keep doing that to me?"

She was not going to be so easily put off. Nothing new about that.

She said: "We talked about something in my workshop today, Jackie, and it's amazing how it applies to you. Your problem is, you can't stand to think about making a commitment to stop doing something *forever*—not even something that's eating your liver. But you don't have to think about it like that. Just think about something you know you can handle. Listen to this—"

She pulled some pages out of her purse. She had it all written down, which wasn't actually unheard-of, either. Besides the phone number, she often left him words of wisdom planted inside whatever he was reading, or sticking out of the slit in his shorts in the bureau drawer.

"Stop *trying* to see the big picture," she said. "You can't see the future—with or without a drink—you can only really see what's *right now*." Then she started to read from her notes: "It's like driving a car at night," she read. "You can only see as far as your headlights, but you can make the whole trip that way. You don't have to see where you're *going*. You don't need to know your destination or see everything you will pass along the way. You just have to see—"

"Whoa. Just *whoa*!" he said. "Don't get mad, but—are you fucking *crazy*?" He knew he was pushing his luck—Cassandra hated it when he got vulgar; her father had a mouth like a leaky sewer— but he was getting a little angry himself. A little *more* angry.

"Come on, Jackie" she said, "don't tell me you don't see the analogy. If you just don't have a drink on this one day—"

"Don't talk to me about 'analogies' when you're talking crazy," Jackie said, maybe a little louder than before. "You're saying, if you're driving at night, *you don't have to see where you're going*? Cassandra—how are you going to make a whole trip if you don't know where you're going? And why would I want to go through the only life I'm ever going to live without seeing *everything* along the way? How can you sit there—"

"I didn't say you don't *know* where you're going!" she said, and she was a little louder now, too; just a hint of frustration darkened by desperation creeping in. "Of course you know where you're *going*, but if you're driving, say, from here to Albany, you don't have to be able to *see*."

"Albany!" he said. "Why in the sweet name of Jesus would I want to drive to *Albany*? Do you hear yourself? Every time we get on this subject you get a little crazy, but this is world-class crazy!"

"God damn you," she said (without an exclamation point; she was determined not to lose her cool). "Don't pretend you don't know what I'm talking about. It's a *metaphor*—"

"Whoa again!" he said. He walked over to her—leaving his drink behind—and leaned in to her face, bracing himself on the arms of the chair.

"We are not at Yale Grad School, me and you, Cassie. I'm jus' a ol' country boy..." Usually she loved it when he played hillbilly, but he could see it wasn't going to work tonight, so he let it go.

Giving her his most direct *I-really-mean-this* look, right in the eyes, he took his hands off the chair and clasped them in front of his face, an unnatural few inches away from hers.

"Do you really want to make me shame myself here and say I don't know the difference between a metaphor and a simile and... and a *nanalogy*?" Sometimes he tripped over a word when he got worked up.

He straightened up and stepped back. Now he spread his arms out in a parody of a rustler surrendering.

"If you want to yell at me because I treasure the God-given right to have a drink or twenty, all right; I'm used to that. Yell away; nobody deserves it more than me. But don't talk to me about some dark night of the soul in *Albany*, for Christ's sake! Thinking about *Albany* is gonna drive me to doubles faster than you can hide the Jack Daniel's!"

She didn't say anything for a minute. He went back to his drink, stepped over to the kitchen counter and added some ice cubes before topping it off. He hadn't offered her anything. He knew better.

"Okay," she said. "Maybe that's not the best way to put it. I actually got that out of a book about writing, but I thought it applied."

"A *writing* book?" Jackie said. "Jesus Christ, Cassie, we're not talking about 'writing.' We're talking about *wronging*!" He stood tall and straight, put on his best mock-Moses face, and pointed at her imperiously. "You're *wronging* me, Cassandra Sullivan, and God will punish you for that!"

He thought that might make her laugh. It didn't.

"Okay; I get it," she said. She hadn't stood up—that was a good sign—but she was leaning forward on the couch as far as she could

"You don't want to hear me," she said. "Well, God damn it, you're *going* to hear me or you're going to have to throw me out bodily. Is that what you want? You want to show me who's boss and show me you can hit harder than my father did? Good luck, because you can't."

That water was way too murky for Jackie, so he just said, "Okay," not loud at all. "Good. I want to hear you. Come on. Let's have it all. Hit me with your best shot." He was pacing around the room now. Her eyes followed him, but she didn't move.

"I hate it when you do that," she said.

"You hate a lot of things I do when you get in this mood," he said, coming to a full stop. "How come this *mood* always seems to coincide with my fourth or fifth drink? You may think that's coincidence but I think you do it on purpose."

She ignored that. "I'm not going to *hit* you with anything," she said, really cool again. Deadly cool. "I'm not even trying to tell you what to think. I'm just trying to show you some different *ways* of thinking. Can you listen for about forty seconds?"

Jackie spread his arms and opened his eyes wide; making himself as totally vulnerable as he could possibly be without actually feeling that way.

"Go," he said.

"Just imagine a little picture frame," she said. "Tiny. One-inch."

"Hold up a minute," he said. "One inch high or one inch wide? Or is it a square frame, like for... a tiny Polaroid?"

She just stared at him for a minute. (He knew it wasn't a whole minute, but it could seem a whole lot longer than that when Cassie stared. Those eyes weren't just luminous. They also talked very loud, or they could be stone silent, and the silent eyes were the ones you didn't ever want to see. Like now.)

"Forget about anything that won't fit into that frame, and stop trying to imagine the whole rest of your life. Forget about tomorrow, or even an hour from now. You just concentrate on what you can see in a one-inch frame. Just *right now*.

"Maybe you can see pouring out the rest of that stupid drink in your hand, for instance," she said. "You can see that, and that's not so scary, is it? You've poured out a few drinks in your time. Spilled one in my lap at the party last week, remember that? Probably not. Lots of things you don't remember, Jackie. Doesn't that *worry* you?"

"Of course it doesn't worry me," he lied. "Let's talk about things I *do* remember. *That* worries me." He loved it when he was quick with words like that.

She just shook her head. Then she said, "Just think about the little frame, Jackie. Think about the satisfaction of moments so small that you can actually *control* them. Just do that, and live with that little moment. One moment after another.

"Then take me to bed and make love to me," she said. "That's just one little moment. You can see that in the frame."

He had to interrupt. "*One little moment* in bed? I can do a lot better than that," he said, and he leered.

"I got a better idea." He was pacing again, his drink in his hand, the other arm swinging as he structured a scenario in the air.

'That's good, that part about making love," he said. "But instead of looking through your little frame, I'll get out the Polaroid camera and look through that. How's zat? We'll make some souvenirs of this wonderful night when I couldn't see past my headlights. Or when I was on the road in a '52 Buick with a short in the wiring. Which is gonna make my headlights cut out and turn everything pitch dark every few minutes. So I miss the turnoff and wind up in Poughkeepsie. Or maybe in *Schenectady*; that'd be even worse, wouldn't it?

"This night when I'm supposed to be looking at life through rose-colored frames that only show me life one fuckin' inch at a time, which isn't much, now is it, Cassandra? That's what you want? Life in one-inch bites? And you don't dare look beyond the headlights to see what's around you? That's *stoopid.*"

"Don't *ever* call me stupid, Jackie," she said. "I'm not *stupid.*" She was on her feet now, and it was her turn to lean in to *his* face.

"That's Jackie *Daniel's* talking," she said, "and I'm trying not to listen. But you're making it *Very. Fucking. Hard.*"

Even Jackie knew he should shut up when she said *fucking*. She was never casual with the word. She even pronounced the *g*, very clearly. He knew, but at the moment he didn't give a damn. He was mad, and it was time for the big gun.

Time to roll out the sarcasm.

"Okay; just listen to *me* for a minute now," he said, stepping back so he could wag his finger in her face. "You know Paddy McGovern. Last of the great old-time Irish saloon-keepers, right? Well, what you don't seem to know is *McGovern's Law*. So I'm going to tell you. It's Paddy's contribution to human wisdom, and it's infallible. That's why it's called a *Law*.

"It goes like this: '*Research shows... that 100% of the people who don't ask for your advice... don't want it.*'

"You got that, Cassandra Sullivan of headlight-and-picture-frame wisdom? Do you see how you are wasting that wisdom tonight by planting it where nobody asked you for it? Here," he said, digging into his pocket and going for the big finish.

"Here. Here's a quarter. Call someone who cares."

She glared. At first she didn't say anything, but her face did the job. Her skin did, actually. It got even whiter. Except in her eyes. They developed little red dots in the center. His big finish had made its point.

He really, really wanted to erase the tape.

Cassandra leaned down to pick up her purse. She stood very straight and looked at his eyes. "I'm not even going to say good night," she said very evenly. "Why should I wish you a good night? You're *pathetic*, and you're just going to get *more* pathetic. I'm not going to waste a wish on you."

"Be careful going home," he said, turning to walk back to the bar on his kitchen counter. "Those cheap headlights and that little tiny frame can limit your vision. You've got great boobs but very limited vision, Cassandra."

Uh oh.

Too far.

The hand that didn't hold her purse had picked up a cheap plastic glass. She deliberately missed his head when she threw it, but her point was made.

"You go to hell, Jackie!" she said. "Just go to hell!" And she was gone.

Jackie stood—swayed—for a moment and then raised his glass to the closed door.

"Listen; this is important," he said, a little too cheerfully for the empty room. "McGovern's Law doesn't apply to that last advice you gave me, about going to hell. I was gonna do that anyway.

"Just always remember, Cassandra: 'If at first you don't succeed ... to hell with it. Why make a fool of yourself?

"That's *Jackie's* Law!"

Warsaw, 1980

Ships That Pass in the Morning

There were 506 people, 68 assorted barnyard animals, 10 tanks, 59 weapons—including one machine gun—and one apoplectic director waiting, probably at a cost of several thousand dollars a minute, on a long dirt road in Poland.

They were waiting on the Director of Photography, Buddy O'Connor, who was there—but not really. He had six cameras at his disposal, and—except for the one in a helicopter—he couldn't seem to decide exactly where he wanted them. The scene was for *The Hounds of Hell*, about the beginning of WWII, and refugees were going to be strafed by the Luftwaffe.

Simon Denker, the director of the miniseries, was spitting nails and sharp stones.

"What the *fuck* is going on down there!" he was shouting. He was used to hurry-up-and-wait on a film set, but he was also the executive producer of this picture, and time is money, godammit, time is money! On days like this he spoke only in exclamation points.

"Give me another minute," O'Conner mumbled. Rain the night before had messed up many of his camera placements, and he was not his usual speedy self in deciding on new ones.

Jackie Barron was the Independent Broadcasting Network publicist for the movie, and he was deeply grateful for the absence of press that morning. He and Buddy O'Connor had become friends of a sort during the filming, and Jackie knew his friend was not looking good under pressure.

"Jackie! Could you come here for a minute?" It was Buddy calling softly, and Jackie couldn't begin to guess what use he could be in this situation. Nonetheless, he moved swiftly to the table where O'Connor was making and tearing up endless sketches of cameras and stick figures. There were also, Jackie noticed, a lot of obscene doodles on the pages.

"Jackie, could you do me a favor, please?"

"Name it, you got it. But I'm not an authority on camera placement."

"It's not funny, Jackie. I can't concentrate on what I'm doing here; I need you to do something for me. Get to one of the field phones and call the production office, see if they've heard from Gretchen's driver."

"Gretchen's coming to the set today?

"No, Jackie, she's not. Because she's not here and never has been. Never. You don't even know who she is. Leave it at that; I'll explain later. Just go make the call. And after you make it—you never heard that name before in your life. Understand?"

Jackie did *not* understand, but he wasn't going to hang around waiting for explanations. The director could be heard swearing and demanding to know what the fuck O'Connor was doing talking to the fucking *publicity guy* at a time like this.

"Just leaving," Jackie shouted, and did.

"I'm getting there, Simon," Buddy said. "Just give me a few more minutes. I'm having trouble getting all these changes straight in my head so we're getting the best coverage."

"What are you talking about? We're not getting *any* coverage! Some of these extras are old people; they're gonna die before you make up your mind! Just *give* me something!"

"Working on it, Simon. Believe me—I'm working on it."

Buddy O'Connor was indeed working on it—and casting glances behind him to see if Jackie Barron was on his way back yet. When the publicist came into view Buddy stopped pretending to concentrate on his work. He was concentrating on his emissary.

"Everything's cool," Jackie said. "That ... uh ... *passenger* who was never here made it to the airport on time and her plane's probably loading right now. And I'm sorry if you guys had a fight."

Buddy O'Connor glowered at him.

"Don't get upset," Jackie said hastily. "What I mean is, I'm glad there couldn't have been a problem between you and this person because you never even heard of this person. If this person even exists. Or whatever you want me to mean, Buddy. Just give me a little guidance."

"Go away," Buddy said. "I'm about to set a new world's record for choreographing six cameras. We'll talk about it later."

Buddy O'Connor did a brilliant job with his cameras, making up a lot of the time his indecision had cost the unit, and Simon Denker wasn't mad at him any more.

That was fortunate, because when Buddy's wife, Maureen, showed up during the lunch break, she found everybody happy. Including and especially her husband, who was properly pleased and surprised by her appearance, even though he'd known she was on her way ever since the production office gave him a heads-up before dawn that morning.

Maureen had decided she deserved a little vacation, and so she had flown from LA to Rome a few days earlier. From there she flew to Dubrovnik to see the seaside, and then—since she was in the neighborhood—she decided to ignore her husband's rule about not coming to locations, and flew in to Warsaw to surprise him. She did, however, remember to call the production office at the last minute, so they could send a car to the airport for her. As soon as she hung up the production secretary very wisely ruined the surprise.

At lunch with the crew, Maureen chattered on about her flights, and her purchases, and told of a funny coincidence on the way from the airport.

"My driver honked and waved at a company car going the other way, with a girl in the back. I guess they didn't know she was leaving or they could've done it all in one trip; my driver could have taken her to the airport when he came to pick me up. Was it one of your stars?"

Jackie broke the silence. "No," he said. "I think she's a hairdresser who came in from LA to help out for a few days. I'm not even sure what her name was."

"Well, I'll tell you," Maureen said, "she's a redhead and she's gorgeous enough to be an actress."

That covered the subject pretty well. For the rest of the day Buddy O'Connor was a totally focused, totally involved, consummate professional.

And within a half-hour, thanks to the mysterious film-unit grapevine, word was around that Buddy's wife had arrived. It was just as well that she never again mentioned the redhead in the other car, since not one of the eighty-six people who made up the permanent crew could remember anything about the girl.

New York, 1955

That's What Friends Are For

Jackie Barron and Mickey O'Hare, who had made the drive to New York from Los Angeles with him, had come to the party on West End Avenue together.

The difference was, Jackie stood at the makeshift bar by himself. This was not unusual behavior for Jackie at parties. He wasn't good at mingling.

Mickey, on the other hand, always made an exploratory tour of the room when he arrived at a party. The room at this one had once been elegant; by 1955 its age was showing. The hostess was an actress he had met at an audition. Her age was not showing.

Jackie watched, fascinated—he had given up on being envious—as Mickey gave his undivided attention to every attractive woman on the premises, one at a time, carefully devoting only slightly less time to those he wasn't interested in taking home. Bypassing the less-attractive could be insulting; women tended to notice things like that, and Mickey hated to accidentally insult anyone.

Unlike Jackie, meeting people, male or female, came easily to Mickey. Most unattached women present would have checked him out as soon as he walked in, as would most of those with boyfriends. His awareness of this had nothing to do with vanity or ego. His looks were not something he took credit for.

Conversation—about pretty much anything—was of equal importance in his success with women, and it was something he obviously enjoyed. This was a talent that sometimes surprised people, since nobody expected it in a hard-bodied, one-time Golden Gloves champion.

After paying his respects to each guest, Mickey withdrew to the bar by the door to join Jackie and consider the evening's prospects. The leading contender for his further attention was an actress with cxploding hair, hypnotic eyes and a wicked smile.

"How you doing, Barron," Mickey said. Calling other men by their last name was an unfortunate habit left over from the Army, but he hadn't managed to break it yet.

The question was not rhetorical. At twenty, Jackie was five years his friend's junior, and a virgin. Mickey kept an encouraging eye on his efforts to terminate that unwelcome condition.

For Jackie, this was easier said than done. With friends of either sex he was quick, open and funny. With people he didn't know—particularly women he was attracted to—it was a little different.

He wasn't anti-social, just shy—and nothing about him inspired love at first sight. His hair was the color of fresh rust, his eyes were hidden behind horn-rimmed glasses, and some of the sexier full-figured women in the room outweighed him.

"Oh, I'm doing great," he said. "I've talked to three different girls for three minutes each. Then they excused themselves to go wait their turn with you. Breaks my usual record by two minutes each. I get worth-by-association, Mickey: I'm with O'Hare so I must be okay. For three minutes."

He was exaggerating a little; it was part of a bantering game he and Mickey had slipped into, with Jackie playing the contemplative intellectual and Mickey the good-timing lady-killer. Actually, the girl from Douglass College had been delighted in meeting Jackie. He was the only one she'd ever known besides herself who liked Shaw better than Shakespeare, and she had hastily written out her address when her date went to take a leak.

"Oh, come on, Barron; you—"

"You know, Mick, I think we know each other well enough now that you could stop calling me *Barron*. Makes me sound like a desert."

"Sorry; sorry. Bad habit. I'll try to do better. What was your nickname when you were a kid?"

"I didn't have one. I wouldn't answer to '*Red*,' and thank God nobody ever called me '*Four-eyes*' or said 'Hey, *Skinny!*'"

"Well ... '*skinny*' would have just been a description, not an insult. How much *do* you weigh?"

"Hundred and twenty."

"And how tall are you?"

"About five-eight and a half."

"Jesus, Barron—either gain twenty pounds or shrink two inches. You make Sinatra look fat."

"Ah, that's why women love you, Mick. You got a sense of humor that would make a turtle laugh."

"I'm not exactly sure what that means," Mickey said. "I have—"

"Stop it! Stop it!"

The muffled scream came from downstairs, and Mickey O'Hare was halfway down those stairs before anyone else realized anything was wrong.

A black teenager was running out the door when Mickey got to the lobby. He recognized the girl on the floor as Marlene Anderson, a transplanted Texan headed for the party.

"Stop him!" she said. "Sumbitch has got my purse! I'll kill him!"

Mickey leaned over her, almost without breaking stride. "Are you all right?"

"Yes! Just *stop* him!"

Mickey was through the door and on the sidewalk by the time she finished speaking. The teenager was running up the block across Riverside Drive. He was no match for Mickey, who caught up with him in the darkness of Riverside Park.

Overwhelming the boy was not a problem, and Mickey had him pinned to the ground when he felt someone land on his back. Hands were wrestling with his arm. Pinning the boy down by his neck, Mickey turned to see his attacker.

It was Jackie Barron. He had carefully taken off his glasses, placed them on the grass and then, not exactly able to distinguish one scuffling figure from another without them, leapt into the fray to help his friend.

"God *dammit*, Barron, that's *my* arm! Just get off me! I've got him!"

Jackie Barron rolled off and Mickey turned both the boy's arms up behind his back, hauling him to his feet. "You get her purse," he said to Jackie, who first found his glasses and then found the purse.

The rest of the encounter became a different kind of drama. A few others from the party had arrived, but

Mickey waved them back to the sidewalk. Only he and Jackie were actually dealing with the boy, who looked to be fifteen or sixteen. He was crying and pleading for a break.

"I didn't hurt her," he said. "Swear to God I didn't hurt her! I never done nothing like this before, man. Please don't call the cops. You'll kill my mother. Okay? Okay?"

It went on like that for a while. Mickey—who had been in a few scrapes with the law in his own teens—alternately lectured and threatened the boy.

"What do you think?" he asked Jackie. They were discussing pros and cons of turning him loose when Marlene Anderson appeared, smacked the teenager in the face and said, "*Nigger sonofabitch!*"

In unison, Mick and Jackie said "*Hey! Hey! Hey*!" And everything changed. Later it wouldn't make a lot of sense to either of them, but they actually apologized to the mugger.

Finally, after considerable consideration, Mickey adopted his fiercest look, shook a finger in the boy's face, took his name and address off his school ID card—to do what with, he had no idea—and sent him away at a dead run with a warning that "I'll personally bust your ass if I ever see you here again."

As they walked back toward the others, Jackie said "Well, this should make me the total buffoon, if anybody ever doubted it. I'm comical for grabbing the wrong arm and pitiful because it didn't make any difference."

"Oh, shut up," Mickey said. "We got the guy, that's all anybody needs to know. Besides, you were a tiger. If I hadn't been around you'd have got him yourself." They both knew better than that, but it was nobody else's damn business. Intention counted.

And Mickey wasn't going to call his friend—who never had a nickname—just *Barron* anymore.

"C'mon, Tiger," he said. "There's hope for you yet."

New York, 1970

Reach Out and Touch

At about ten past one on a long Saturday night, Jackie Barron decided he was tired of sitting in the Savor Bar and drinking alone. The odds were against anyone he knew stopping in here, especially at this hour, and no one in the place seemed interested in striking up a conversation. Going home was clearly the logical move.

By a quarter past one he had convinced himself that calling Gina Rossi wasn't as bad an idea as he knew it really was. Fifteen past one wasn't too late to call. It would be okay even if it was seventeen past by the time he got to the phone booth and dug her number out of his little black book. (He found it properly silly that his phone book really was little and black.)

The hour wouldn't be too late. The year might. He hadn't seen her for almost a year, but that wasn't really his fault. He'd liked Gina a lot, but she finally became absolutely unreasonable about his drinking.

The night she sent him on his way hadn't been horrible—he was pretty sure a few vulgarities had been exchanged—but he was also sure it hadn't been *that* bad.

Nothing wrong with a friendly call now, just to ask how she's doing. And if she invited him to come over ... that would be okay, too.

Getting to the phone booth at the back of the bar wasn't the bad part of what followed. He managed the journey with only one misstep, bumping into a solitary drinker. The guy on the stool was too busy with darker thoughts to complain about being bumped, so Jackie proceeded. Finding a dime to drop into the coin slot was no problem; it just meant taking another couple of minutes to pick up the rest of his change from the floor.

The bad part of what followed was his little black book. It was a perfectly reliable phonebook, but it wasn't in his jacket pocket, where it was supposed to be. The worst part of what followed was that it wasn't in any other pocket, either.

"Shit," he thought. When heads at the bar turned towards him he realized that he hadn't just thought it.

"My phone book," he told the three sets of eyes that were looking at him. Only the bartender's eyes seemed interested in Jackie's problem. Or maybe the bartender was just wary of customers who said *Shit!* out loud when they weren't talking to anyone.

Jackie made his way back to the stool where he had been sitting. He examined the floor under and around the stool. Nothing but a few cigarette butts and some burnt matches. (None of them his. Jackie always used an ashtray, even in a bar where nobody knew him.)

"Did I leave my phone book on the bar?" he asked the bartender. "Little black thing. There's kind of a chip out of the spine and some cracks in the cover. It's pretty old. And it's not real leather. You know?"

The bartender carefully removed what remained of Jackie's drink and put it with the dirty glasses. "Yeah, I know," he said. "And no, you didn't. Maybe you didn't carry it tonight. Maybe —"

"No, no," Jackie said. "Nope. Never go out without it. I'm not good at remembering numbers. Are you good at that? Not me, boy. Sometimes I forget my own number. Do you ever do that? It's embarrassing; you just—"

"I tell you what you ought to do, pal," the bartender said. "You ought to retrace your steps. Okay? Do you remember where you been?"

"Yeah. Good idea. I'm going back. That's it. Are we all square here?"

The bartender had already taken the price of Jackie's drink from his money on the bar before suggesting he move along. "Got it," he said. "That last one's on me."

Jackie left a generous tip and headed back to McGovern's Tavern, his second home, which was only a few blocks away. His phone book had to be there, because now he remembered taking it out and calling his friend Flip, who wasn't interested in joining him for a drink. Neither, he remembered, was Jerry. Or Elena; her answering machine said she was in Atlanta with *Cabaret*. He didn't give more than a passing thought to Cassie, who was married and all. It had not been a good night for telephone calls.

Going back to McGovern's was the right move. Paddy McGovern was gone for the evening, but Al the Bartender interrupted Jackie as soon as he began describing the missing phonebook.

"I think this note's for you," Al said. "I don't know the guy who left it; he just said give it to the guy who lost his phonebook. That would be you, right?"

Jackie, the weight of the world lifted from his shoulders, grabbed for the note. He got it on the second grab.

The note read: *This is some phonebook you got here. Judy Garland's phone number? Cherokee McNair's phone number? Alex Venture? You know a bunch of stars. I bet these addresses and phone numbers would be worth some money to someone. Maybe you should give me a call.*

Pretty chatty for a ransom note, Jackie thought. And it was signed *Ponce de Leon*. Probably not his real name. Jackie's hand was trembling now, but not from the Jack Daniel's he had consumed. The Garland number was there because one of her husbands was an old friend of Jackie's. Alex Venture had been his friend long before he won an Emmy for his new series. Cherokee McNair had been Jackie's girlfriend for a while, but not until long after she'd starred as "Changa, the Jungle Girl" on television. She would kill him if he let some freak have her unlisted number. She'd already had to change it three times.

Those weren't the only numbers in there that shouldn't get out. He was a publicist at the Indy Broadcasting Network, and working with stars was his job. Sometimes he wrote their numbers in his personal phone book. He knew he shouldn't, but it seemed like a harmless conceit. It was fun having those numbers. Like having an imaginary playmate.

Jackie dialed the call from McGovern's phone booth. It was picked up on the first ring.

"This is the legendary Ponce de Leon," the voice said. "What can I do you for?"

"I'm the guy who lost —" Jackie began.

"Yeah, I kind of thought you would be," the voice said. "I been sitting here dying to call Farrah Fawcett but LA's long-distance, and I didn't want to run up my bill. Unless you prefer it that way. What do you think? Should I call her up?"

"I get your meaning." Jackie's voice was carefully controlled and surprisingly sober. "How much?"

"Well, let's see," Ponce said. "You got at least twenty hot numbers in here. Hundred dollars apiece sound about right?"

"Senor de Leon," Jackie said, "you're as crazy as he was. Am I made out of money? Look at those names again. Then look at mine; it's in the front of the book. Do I sound like somebody you ever heard of? Or does it seem more like maybe I'm their paperboy? Or the guy who walks their dogs?"

Jackie gave him a moment to think it over, then said: "Let's get real here, okay? You want $2,000 for that phonebook? How about you give *me* the $2,000; I'll deliver Cherokee McNair to your door. Why not. I'm sure she made you horny when you were about twelve, but she hasn't worked steady since the '50s faded away." (Cherokee McNair was a perfectly respectable lady in spite of the artfully tattered costumes she'd worn as Changa, and Jackie couldn't "deliver" her anywhere. But it felt good to talk like a hard guy.)

"Bring me the book back here at McGovern's right now and I'll scrape up $50 for your trouble."

"Oh, come on, man! Fifty dollars? You're insulting me! And how do I know you won't have your Irish lynch-mob waiting?"

"All right," Jackie said. "I'll try for a hundred. I think I can come up with that. And I'll meet you at Hamburger Heaven on 71st and Broadway. They're open all night, but it's got to be *right now*, and you don't copy down any fucking numbers. Be there in ten minutes or don't bother; I'll let the police handle it. Time starting *now*." Jackie had never played tough before; it was fun.

"Jesus Christ," the man who called himself Ponce said. "Why you wanna be like that? I was just jerking your chain, man. Hundred bucks is fine, and you know it's worth it. I'm doing you a favor. I'll see you at Hamburger Heaven; ten minutes. I'll even buy you a burger if you want; no hard feelings. I hate hard feelings, man."

"No burger," Jackie said. "And I guess no hard feelings. It's my own dumb fault. But just remember—if you ever try to bother anybody in that book—now I've got *your* number, too. You clear on that?" Ponce was clear.

Jackie still had a folded fifty in his wallet, and Al the Bartender, shaking his head in open disapproval, gave him another fifty from the cash register. He entered the sum on Jackie's page in the Account Book where a tab was run for the bar's regulars

Jackie found Ponce, true to his word, sitting with the neighborhood streetwalkers and pot-peddlers who made Hamburger Heaven a neighborhood hangout for late-night breaks. The air of non-violent decadence always appealed to Jackie and it seemed particularly appropriate for this night's transaction.

When the exchange was made, Jackie passed on the hamburger. But he did have a coffee with Ponce—real name Larry-Something—who turned out to be a singularly unimposing young man with acne-scarred cheeks and a nose veined by lines as red as a highway map.

"Don't go away mad, man," Larry Something said. "I'm not a bad guy. You want to call a couple of your friends, we'll go have a taste somewhere? I know a good after-hours joint in the neighborhood." He flourished the bills Jackie had handed him. "My treat," he said.

Jackie passed up the invitation and left. It wasn't even 2:30 yet, so he stopped at the corner to take out the phonebook once again. Gina Rossi answered on the third ring.

And hung up before he could finish saying "Hi, Gina; it's Jackie Ba—"

New York, 1984

On the Other Hand, Sometimes a Cigar *Really* Isn't

The novelist Elmore Leonard says that he tries to "leave out the parts that people skip." Jackie Barron appreciated that because he was an obsessive reader who skipped many things. These included chase scenes, torture scenes, landscape descriptions, most character descriptions, details of the whaling industry, and—pretty near always—dream scenes.

Skipping ahead was not always so easy in life. It wasn't possible to turn the page, or hit Fast Forward, when a friend said: "You won't *believe* the dream I had last night!"

Jackie was always tempted to say: "You're probably right, so there's not much point in telling me, is there?"

He felt that way right now, sitting in his living room with Cassandra Sullivan. Over the years they had been lovers, and then friends, and then lovers, and then friends again. Like that. This was a friends period, so he settled for a non-committal: "Uh huh."

"It was awful," she said, "but really interesting and probably important."

Jackie doubted both those judgments, but kept his silence.

"I was in this big, foggy space," she said. "That kind of no-place place you get into in dreams. It was dark and I couldn't see, and then my father stepped out of the fog in a trench coat, like Humphrey Bogart."

"I've got the picture," Jackie said.

"You know I have these ambivalent feelings about my father, but just looking at him in this dream I could tell that death agreed with him. It was so incredibly real, Jackie, and I knew—I just *knew*— that he was really sorry—sorry he ignored me so much; sorry he never approved of me. It was going to be the breakthrough we never had."

"I'm very happy for you," Jackie said. "That's a lovely dream. Now can we —"

"But then you know what happened?"

Jackie shrugged. "He took you in his arms and gave you a big hug and cried?"

"He was going to," she said. "I *know* he was going to. But all of a sudden—you know how dreams are—my bitch mother was alive, too, and standing between us."

"Uh-oh," Jackie said.

"Wherever he moved she moved too, and she kept getting closer to him all the time. Finally she was right up against him and—oh, God; I can't *stand* it! I don't know if I can tell you!"

Jackie very quickly said: "That's okay, Cassie; you don't have to! You're entitled to your privacy. Now can we —"

"She started unbuttoning my father's pants, Jackie! It was disgusting. I *knew* what she was going to do, and I knew that was what kept him from bonding with *me*! She didn't want *anybody* else in his life, not even his *daughter*. Sex was her weapon! It was just finally all so clear!"

"Well," Jackie said, "that's... uh... some dream. Did you keep watching while they... did it?"

"No! God, Jackie, I couldn't imagine that when they were alive and I'm sure not going to imagine it now. Not even in a dream. I did what a daughter ought to do. I woke up."

"And I for one am damn glad you did. A sight like that can mark even a middle-aged woman for life. I know I —"

"Watch who you're calling middle-aged," she said.

"Sorry. What I meant to say was: even a woman at the *peak* of her own sexual powers, okay?"

"I'll accept that," Cassie said.

"It's just that I know how competitive you are with your mother, dead or alive. Seeing her getting your father naked might have driven you prematurely bonkers!"

Cassie shook her head. "That's all right," she said. "Make fun of me. But it was a *significant* dream, and it could make changes in my whole attitude towards life."

"Good," Jackie said. "I'm sure life would appreciate that."

"Oh, come on! Didn't you ever have a dream that you knew had *meaning*?"

"Matter of fact," Jackie said, "I did have a disturbing symbolic dream last week. You were in it."

"Really?" she said. "Tell me!"

"I was about thirty, which I know because we were in the Riverside Drive apartment, after we broke up the second time. We were standing real close, and you were still really mad at me."

"That would be the 1964 breakup," Cassie said.

"The point is, I knew I *had* to make love to you, just one more time."

"You've said that every time I've seen you for twenty years, Jackie."

"Please. We hadn't said a word, but I took a cigar out of my pocket and I touched it to your lips. And then I very gently pushed it into your mouth. In a nice way."

"A cigar? What on earth were you doing with a cigar?"

"It was a dream, Cassie. Will you let me finish?"

"Go ahead."

"Now the cigar was in your mouth, and I pushed it in a little further, but it had gotten lit somehow—you know how dreams are. All of a sudden your mouth was full of smoke. You got really mad—I remember you called me a pig—and you spit it all out."

"Well, what do you —"

"May I finish, please? This is the important part. You looked down at the mess in your hand and you said: 'You call this a *cigar*? This is more like a *cigarette stub*. My new boyfriend has a *much* bigger cigar. His is *Cuban*, you know!'

"First I was hurt, and then I was furious, but when I grabbed it out of your hand ... you were right. It was just a cigarette. A Pall Mall. I said something stupid like: 'Well... it's a very *nice* cigarette.' And you sneered and you said: 'No, it isn't *nice*. Look at it. You don't even use a *filter*!' And that's when I woke up."

"Whoa. Did you really dream that?" she asked.

"Okay—not exactly. I definitely dreamed I was with you in the old apartment. And I wanted you so bad I ached all over. All that's true," he said.

"I made up the part about the cigar."

Cassie was shaking her head. "You really are a filthy old man, Jackie," she said. "But I wouldn't change you for the world. And that goes for your little cigar, too."

Hutchins, Tennessee, 1947

The Farewell Tour of Tex Ritter's Sidekick

The boy was twelve years old and he was moving on. Time to leave Hutchins, Tennessee, the Smoky Mountain town where he lived with his Aunt Hazel and Uncle Max. It was the only town he had ever lived in.

His name was Jonathan Edward Barron but everybody called him Jackie, and probably always would. His grandmother used to say they should prob'ly call him John because he was the *oldest* little boy she ever saw, but he just wasn't a John. *No*; she used to say, *he's our Jackie, and that's just all they is to it.*

Growing up with his aunt and uncle and sometimes with his grandmother never seemed odd to the boy. Whatever "the Depression" was, he had been born in it. He knew it meant a lot of people couldn't afford to go around raising children, so people in the family helped each other out. That's just the way it was. It was the only life he had ever known, and they were always nice to him, so he never had any reason to complain.

Now the big war against Hitler and Tojo had been over for two years, and tomorrow morning he would get in the car with his aunt and uncle and they would drive to Los Angeles. His mother had moved out there because women could get good jobs at the defense plants while the men were off being soldiers. Now Jackie could go live with her. He didn't really know her too good, but he used to go visit her sometimes, and he always liked her.

He was moving two thousand miles away to a town with a whole lot more people than Hutchins had—they wasn't but 1300 people in Hutchins. He'd finally live with the mother he didn't hardly know and a stepfather he hadn't never met. That sounded fine to him. Besides which, it wasn't up to him, so they wasn't no reason to fuss about it.

On his last day before leaving Hutchins, Jackie went on a farewell mosey around town. He wasn't unhappy about leaving. Still, he figured he should take a last look at some of the places he would never see again. That seemed like something that somebody in a story would do, and Jackie loved stories. He liked the idea of being in one on this last day.

His first stop was the school, because there was only one schoolhouse in town and it was only a little ways away from his aunt's house. Jackie was disappointed that he didn't feel anything when he looked at it for the last time. He'd liked school all right. Everybody said he was real smart, but he'd had to be careful about that when he was living with his grandparents. (The other grandchildren called them Granny and Daddo, but that sounded like baby-talk to Jackie, so he called them Mama and Daddy, like his aunts did.)

Sometimes Mama thought he sounded like he was gettin' all stuck-up when he talked too much about what he was learning, and she would say: *Boy, don't you try to raise above your upbringins!* Jackie understood that she just meant *don't be a show-off!* so he tried not to be.

His grandparents were sorta *country*, and when Jackie was five years old he lived with them on the far edge of town. They kept pigs in the back, and they still used an outhouse and had a well for water. Jackie knew that embarrassed his Aunt Hazel sometimes—Uncle Max had a real good job and him and her lived on Main Street and had a real nice bathroom and water inside the house. Living out in the country with Mama and Daddy hadn't bothered Jackie none—except when he had to go to the outhouse at night in the winter. That was cold and scary.

While he was still saying goodbye to the schoolhouse, Jackie pulled out the wallet he got for Christmas and took out his school picture. It was in black and white but he could still see the freckles, and a shock of hair flopped down over his forehead. He hated it—who wouldn't. He looked like a *kid*, and he hated being just a kid. He pulled up a loose chunk of concrete on the walkway to the school and put the picture under it. Somebody would find it someday and wonder who in the world that used to be.

He walked slowly as Main Street went upwards, and he waved goodbye to the water tower that stood on top of the hill. Him and his best friend had always talked about climbing the ladder that led to the top of the tower, but they never did. They talked about doing a lot of things that they never did.

At the bottom of the other side of the hill he came to the First Baptist Church. There were all kinds of people in Hutchins—not just Baptists. There were Methodists and Presbyterians, too. Just outside of town there were even Holy Rollers, who had revivals in a big ol' tent and everybody talked in tongues and ... well ... rolled around some. Jackie had snuck into one of their meetings once, and stayed until he got scared that they would make him talk funny, too. They called themselves Pentecostals, but everybody knew they were really Holy Rollers. All the churches seemed to be talking about the same God and Jesus, but the First Baptist was the church he had always gone to, and all his people said it was the right one.

He stopped in front of the red-brick building and imagined the painting of the River Jordan that covered the wall behind the water tank where the preacher did baptisms. Brother Thomas had dunked him in over his head there last year and announced that he'd been born again. Jackie thought that was kind of funny because he couldn't swim and he felt like he was being born again when he came out of *any* kind of deep water alive. He hadn't felt any different after being baptized, but he acted like he did. It was what you were supposed to do.

Traveling on past the church, Jackie came to the one spot he knew he would miss most. He came to the Capital Theater, where every Saturday there was a double feature with two cowboy pictures and a bunch of cartoons for a dime. It was also where the great movie star and country singer Tex Ritter had come to town and done his show one Saturday, and they secretly picked out Jackie to be part of the program. Tex Ritter's helper put a King of Hearts playing card in Jackie's shirt pocket and made him promise not to tell anybody.

Later, when Tex Ritter did a magic trick in his show, he picked a boy "at random" from the audience—*yes, you; you little red-haired rascal!*—and Jackie climbed up onto the stage, his brown corduroy knickers making that *shick-shick* sound with every step. Another boy had pulled a King of Hearts card out of the deck Tex Ritter had in his hands, and the singing cowboy had made it magically disappear.

When he told Jackie to check his pocket, why—*there it was*!

Since Jackie figured that only a magician or a mind-reader could know that getting up on the stage was his secret dream, he had no trouble keeping Tex Ritter's secret about the card. He had never told a soul, and now, on this last day in town, he still wouldn't. People in show-business had to be able to keep each other's secrets.

The Capital Theater was maybe the most important place in his life. He knew there would be plenty of bigger and better picture-shows in Los Angeles, but there would probably never again be a famous singing movie star like Tex Ritter to call him up on stage just like he belonged there. Leaving the Capital Theater was hard.

It was only a short walk from there to the L&N railroad tracks on the edge of town. He used to walk on the tracks out in the country with his granddaddy. They didn't talk much—Daddy wasn't much of a talker; mostly he just smoked his pipe—but they picked up the chunks of coal that fell off the freight trains, and Daddy always said *you're hotter'n a pistol today!* when Jackie found really big chunks. They mostly did it just for the fun of it—Daddy had his pension from the railroad so they weren't poor—and Jackie always liked putting the coal he had picked up into the iron stove that heated their living-room. Mostly, really, he just liked walking the tracks with his granddaddy. Calling him Daddy didn't make him Jackie's real father, but the boy never understood what was so important about a real father anyway.

The other side of the tracks was called Socktown, because that's mostly where the people who worked in the cotton mill lived. Jackie didn't know but one person who lived in Socktown, and she had stopped being his girlfriend a year before, so he didn't figure he needed to go see her.

Just down Cross Street was Johnson's Dry Goods store, where he used to go sometimes at night with his uncle, who was the manager. Uncle Max would be upstairs at his desk and Jackie would be downstairs, with the clothes and kitchen stuff and electric stuff and toys and just about everything else anybody could ever need. Sometimes Jackie used to take a railroad-cap off one of the counters and tuck a bandanna in the back so's it covered his neck, and pretend he was in the desert with the French Foreign Legion, like Gary Cooper or somebody. An empty store at night was a good place to play, but Jackie was really too old for all that stuff now, so he wouldn't much miss it.

Back on Main Street there was the empty lot where the medicine shows set up in the summer, with fiddle-players and funny-men. They would sell Hadacol and other things that were supposed to cure what ails you, but his Uncle Max called them *snake-oil,* and said they was mostly just alcohol and sugar. That made it pretty popular with some of the good ol' boys in town, because you couldn't sell any kind of alcohol anywhere in Jackson County. Jackie didn't want any snake-oil, but he always came early to get a good place to stand at the medicine shows anyway.

On the side of the street where the First National Bank stood on the corner, the old men who came in from the country on Saturdays would hunker down and swap stories while their women did the shopping. Jackie liked being around them, listening to the way they talked, saying things like *I wudden but knee-high to a piss-ant in them days*, or *My mama woulda snatched me bald if I ever talked to her like 'at!* Funny, grown-up things. In his mind he would try to talk the way they did, even though he knew he couldn't talk that way at home without somebody telling him to stop actin' the fool.

Some of the men would go up to the barbershop, which had pool tables in the back room. Jackie wasn't allowed to go back there, but he did anyway.

Out on the sidewalk, mostly the old men would just squat on the corner for hours. They would wrap their arms around their knees and put their feet flat on the sidewalk without leaning back against the wall and never lose their balance. They always thought it was funny when Jackie tried to sit on his heels like that, because he would always fall backwards, and somebody would say *that red-hair boy's goin' ass-over-teakettle agin!* After a little while he had stopped trying. Jackie never could see the sense in keepin' on trying something if you weren't any darn good at it.

The drugstore with the really good walnut sundaes was next door. He would miss playing their pinball machine. Jackie had learned just how much he could lean on it to send the ball where it needed to go without making the machine flash *Tilt*, and he won a bunch of free games. He'd never been very good at sports so he hated the thought of leaving something he was good at.

On his walk he passed a lot of people who recognized him—after all, he had lived here all his life (at least, all of it since he was old enough to remember stuff). A few of them knew he was leaving and weren't sure whether to congratulate him or sympathize with him or what. Mostly they congratulated him, because folks just took it for granted that every boy wanted to be with his mother. Jackie guessed that made sense, and he just agreed with whatever they said. He liked it when people looked like they were sad he was leaving.

He slowed down again when he passed the telephone office where Inez ran the switchboard that connected everybody in town with everybody else. Aunt Hazel and Uncle Max's number was 3-0, but if somebody who'd moved to California called up long-distance and nobody was home, Inez could find you no matter where you were. Everybody knew she listened in on the calls—sometimes she would get so excited by something she heard that she would forget herself and break in—but nobody minded. Inez wasn't a mean gossip.

The next stop brought up one of Jackie's silliest and most favorite memories. Miz Grant's little tiny store was called *Good Things*, and it sold what Johnson's Dry Goods store didn't. Miz Grant, who was a really old widow lady—prob'ly fifty; maybe even more—sold books and puzzles and watches and picture-frames and stationery and all kinds of other stuff that women liked, but her store was important to him because that's where he bought his first book.

When he was eight or nine years old his mother started sending him a special allowance of $1 every month from California, and when he got the first dollar he went to see Miz Grant about the book called "Toby Tyler" which he told her was *the one about the boy who runned off with the circus*. He was too old for it now, but in those days it seemed like something he purely *had* to have for his own self. His dollar wasn't quite enough to buy it, and he didn't want to give her *all* his money anyway, so he asked could he open a charge-account like Aunt Hazel had at Johnson's Dry Goods Store. He would give her a twenty-five-cent down-payment and another quarter every month until it was all paid for. Miz Grant said that was the sweetest thing she ever heard of, and of course he could.

Jackie had been very proud of this, but his Aunt Hazel got all upset for some reason. *Do you want people to go around saying we're so stingy you have to open a charge-account and buy your own book?* she said. Then his Uncle Max told her it was really a good thing for the boy to learn about money this way, so he got to keep the book and pay for it a quarter at a time. But his aunt made sure that everybody they knew understood that this was just so he could learn about business, not because they were too mean to buy Jackie that Toby Tyler book.

The farewell tour was over. Heading back to his aunt's house, he stopped off to have a goodbye-talk with his friend Walter Bob Feston. Walter Bob wondered if Jackie's name would be Jackie Hamilton now, since that was his mother's new last name. Jackie said *I reckon*, but it wasn't something he'd thought about much. It wouldn't be up to him anyways.

The boys said goodbye and agreed that they would be friends forever, even though Jackie didn't see how they could be, with him living in California and all.

After his tour he didn't feel as much like someone in a story as he had hoped he would. Leaving didn't seem like all that big a thing to him. Hutchins was nice, but Los Angeles was bigger. And bigger was prob'ly better.

Later on, people told him how hard leaving the only people he'd ever lived with and the only home he'd ever known must have been for him. He was a little embarrassed. The only thing he really regretted was no longer having that Toby Tyler book.

New York, 1961

Third Date

With the hem of Gina Rossi's skirt nearing the panty-line, and Jackie Barron's fingers sliding along her thighs to move it there, it seemed to him that something new and significant was about to happen in their relationship.

The evening—their third together—hadn't started out with anything more significant than dinner at McGovern's Tavern and a ride on the Staten Island Ferry.

That part of the evening was only half new. Their first time together had also been spent at McGovern's, a classic old-school Irish saloon on Columbus Avenue. They had been introduced by Jackie's friend, Norris Carter, who knew her because he was dating Angelica Andrews, her roommate.

"This girl is perfect for you," Norris had assured him. "Child of nature. She'd feel right at home if you took her to McGovern's—although God knows I'll never understand why you would."

"Don't be disrespectful of Paddy McGovern, Norris—I've known him longer than I've known you. And he's a whole lot cheaper than those classy East Side joints where you hang out."

"Well, alright, I suppose I can be a little liberal. We can all meet there for a drink. She'll love it. If you agree with me—and you will—you're on your own after that. You can follow up by taking her to one of those folkie dumps that you love; there's some wannabe hobo down there that the New York Times raved about. Not that a good review in the Times means anything—they loved that unreadable Jack Kerouac novel that you lent me."

"I apologized for that. God knows why I thought a Scott Fitzgerald idolater could find something to like in *On the Road*."

"Don't change the subject; we're talking about Gina Rossi. She's a little mature for me," Norris continued. "Twenty-five if she's a day. But she's petite and full-figured and she has a glorious laugh and I'd probably be all over her myself if I weren't already involved with Angelica."

The thought of Norris being all over any girl who fit any part of that description struck Jackie as more laughable than likely. Norris and the girls who appealed to him—bright young blondes, built like models—were strictly Upper East-Siders, and he was lowering his standards to arrange the double-date for McGovern's only because that was Jackie's home turf.

The exploratory date went well. Gina didn't quite match Jackie drink-for-drink—his, Johnnie Walker Black; hers, red wine—but she held her own. (Wine was a risky choice at McGovern's, but Paddy broke out his private stock for her, in Jackie's honor.)

When Norris and Angelica decided it was time to move on, Gina and Jackie happily waved them goodbye and ordered another round, followed by fish & chips for both.

Jackie was sure he had found a winner in Gina. When the evening ended, and they shared a goodnight kiss at her door, he was even more convinced by the delicate touch of her tongue on the inside of his lower lip.

Since neither of them seemed to have the slightest interest in hiding their interest, they made their next date on the spot.

Jackie had told her how Norris described her, which made her laugh.

"Sounds like me, all right," she said. "We should show our appreciation by proving he's right." So they went to the coffee-house called Gerde's Folk City to hear the "wannabe hobo," Bob Dylan.

They had dinner at The Hip Bagel and coffee at Gerde's. They weren't exactly sure they liked Dylan, but they didn't regret going.

Afterwards they stopped off for a drink or three at McGovern's, and when they got to her door Jackie made it clear that he would love to be invited in. Gina made it clear that she would love it, too, but it wasn't going to happen. Not yet.

"Bear with me, Jackie," she said. "We both know what's likely to happen if you come in. We'd—"

Jackie interrupted with his tongue caressing hers, deeper this time. It was a while before they silently agreed that it was time to stop for a breath.

When they finally—reluctantly—did, Gina said, "Exactly. That's what would happen, only multiplied exponentially."

"Good God," Jackie said. "Who could resist a girl who says things like *multiplied exponentially*? From your lips to God's ear."

"Let's leave my lips and God's ear out of it for the moment, okay?" she said. "We're just starting to walk. Let's warm up a little before we start accelerating."

Jackie wasn't crazy about agreeing, but he did. Just knowing that acceleration was on her mind sent him home happy.

And so, on the following night, the new almost-couple laughed and clung their way through a deliciously romantic 25-minute sea voyage on the ferry. Gina insisted on paying the nickel for her own fare, but Jackie, appalled, said that would emasculate him. Gina, equally appalled, said that damn sure wasn't what she had in mind, and graciously allowed him to spring for the whole dime.

They didn't bother to get off when it docked on Staten Island and by doing so they avoided the extra five cents each that the return trip would have cost them.

"I used to do this when I first moved to New York," he said. "Only in those days I was alone. I pretended I was a plain-clothes pirate."

It was only 10 o'clock when they landed back in Manhattan and took the 7th Avenue IRT subway back uptown, so they stopped off at McGovern's for a drink. They decided that vodka-stingers would be a properly sophisticated way to celebrate their third date. They had more than a few.

When they finally reached Gina's door and Jackie tilted her head up to kiss her, her hand was already in her purse, fishing for her key. They broke the kiss only long enough for her to put the key in the lock. Then Jackie turned her around, kissed her once more, and backed her gently through the door into her apartment and onto her couch.

"Angelica's staying with Norris tonight," she said.

They didn't talk a lot after that. Couldn't, really. Their lips were pretty well fused. His hands explored her breasts and unsnapped her bra. Her hand unbuckled his belt, pulled his zipper down and invaded his jockey shorts.

The silence remained unbroken—except for the occasional moan or *yes!* or *ah!*—until the fingers exploring her thigh were slipping under the elastic of her underwear. At that point, Gina carefully pushed him back a little and put a staying hand on his arm.

She looked him in the eyes and smiled timidly when she said, "Is this a really bad time to tell you that I'm a pretty committed virgin?"

Jackie, stunned, started to pull his own hand back into neutral territory but she grabbed his wrist and held it right where it was.

"I said I'm a virgin," she said. "I didn't say I'm asexual."

"There you go with those awesome words again," Jackie said, still breathing hard. "And the answer to your question is... yeah. This was maybe *not* the best time. You could have—"

"I know, I know, I know," she said mournfully. "I'm sorry!"

Jackie withdrew his entrenched hand and raised it to her cheek.

"No, no. It's okay. There probably hasn't been a... *good* time to say that since you were... oh... thirteen, maybe. But it's all right. We'll work it out."

Gina placed a silencing finger on his lips.

"Tell me if this is okay," she said, sliding off the couch onto the carpet, sliding his shorts down to his ankles and taking him into her mouth.

After a moment in which he couldn't breathe, Jackie said, "*Oh, yes,*" trying not to gasp. "That is all right. That is—*ah!*—definitely all right."

The intimacy of her lips and her tongue—and her eyes when she looked up into his—threw an incongruous song from "My Fair Lady" into his head. There was no place else on earth where he would rather be. No sight besides her eyes that he would rather see. His hands reached down to cup her cheeks and run his fingers through her hair. Along with the *ahs!* and the repetition of *Gina!* he occasionally called out to the Supreme Being.

After the time-out-of-time peaked, after his whole body imploded before flowing into her mouth, he dropped to his own knees—almost losing his balance in the process—and kissed her.

The kiss was wet and slippery and a surprise to both of them. Finally, with a leisurely push, Gina separated herself from him. Shielding her mouth with her fingers when she spoke, she excused herself and went into her bathroom.

When she returned, her face freshly scrubbed, Jackie was back on the couch. His pants were pulled up but still unzipped, and he sat her carefully down beside him.

"That... was gorgeous," he said. "Gorgeous."

She smiled. "You're pretty gorgeous yourself. And I'm sorry about the Restricted Entry. I think it's probably crazy at this point in my life. I'm not exactly a regular at Mass, but here I am—still a good little Italian Catholic girl protecting my good little Italian-Catholic hymen.

"Plus which I'm scared to death of getting pregnant. My father would kill me and Father Anthony would probably help him."

Jackie eased down onto his knees, in the same spot where she had been. He slowly slid both hands up under her skirt once again and respectfully removed her panties before guiding her forward until she was sitting on the edge of the couch.

Spreading her legs, he moved his face into the secluded territory, kissing the inside of each thigh along the way.

"There is no way I'm complaining," he said softly into the welcoming orifice, "but we could use a condom, you know. You wouldn't get pregnant."

His tongue slipped into its natural destination and it was Gina's turn to gasp.

"Shame on you!" she said. "Good Catholic girls... can't... use condoms."

Trying but failing to suppress a giggle, she gasped again and, without thinking, embraced Jackie's head with her upper thighs.

New York, 1984

Thus Spake JackieB

Becoming an irascible, cranky old man had always appealed to Jackie Barron, and nearing fifty he was delighted to discover that it wasn't something he would have work at. It came naturally to him.

Cassandra Sullivan, his sometime lover and almost all the time friend, often brought that out in him, mostly because he knew that *she* knew better than to take him seriously. No matter how serious *he* thought he was.

"There! There! Did you hear that? That's what drives me crazy!" he said.

They were sitting in The Broadcast Grill on West 54th Sreet, and he was pointing to the television set mounted behind the bar. They had moved their occasional lunches to this spot after the closing of McGovern's Tavern, which had been their haunt when they were lovers and Jackie was still an active drunk.

"Where's *what*, Jackie?" she asked. Cassie could feel a tirade coming on, and she knew that—even sober—he was going to pursue his thought, probably talking loud and fast in the process.

"Didn't you hear what she said? That lady on Channel 7 News?"

Cassie, not at all sure where this was going, but certain that it would, said "I think she's talking about something that happened in the O.J. trial yesterday. Do you really care?"

"I don't care what she said about O.J.—but I damn sure care about how she *said* it. She's a professional talker and she put the P-word where it doesn't belong! No wonder this generation is only quasi-literate."

"Okay, Jackie, I'll bite: What did she say?"

"What she said was 'I'll take the proverbial shot in the dark', that's what she said, may her tribe decrease!"

"That just means she's *guessing* about something; what's wrong with that?"

"No, it means she doesn't know what *proverbial* means. Haven't I taught you anything in thirty years?"

"Yes," she said. "You taught me never to say *Fuck you!* when I'm mad at somebody, because that's wishing him something good. You said *Unfuck you!* is the really nasty curse. I've been saying it and confusing hell out of people ever since."

"Good. That's very good. 'Fuck' was always a good word for us. But let's not go into *that.* No, Cassie, the problem is, 'shot in the dark' is just a plain old garden variety cliché—like 'garden variety'. *A stitch in time saves nine'*—that's a proverb. There's no *proverb* about a shot in the dark!"

Cassie leaned back in her chair, prepared for the onslaught.

"A proverb includes a little wisdom, preferably with a little humor. But every time people are about to use a cliché they try to justify it by saying it's *proverbial,*" because that sounds... *meaningful.*"

Cassie liked to think of these moments as *Jackie's got his stridents on,* so she didn't bother trying to interrupt. When he got like this he became thirty again, which actually was appealing to her. She had fond memories—along with infuriating memories—of Jackie at thirty.

“They toss *proverbial* around like teenagers toss around *like*. It’s probably one of the most abused words in the language. Once you start thinking about it you’ll see it and hear it everywhere. It’s second only to *déjà vu* and *literally* and maybe *decimated*.”

“Okay,” she said, “pretend like I asked you to explain, because you’re going to anyway.”

“It’s like this: people go back to a place where they’ve been before, and they’ll get very literary and say ‘Wow—this is really *déjà vu*, isn’t it?’ And the answer is NO. It’s just *remembering* something, because they really *have* been there before. *Déjà vu* is *remembering something that never happened*! It took a songwriter to describe it right. Larry Hart wrote “Where or When,” and it says, ‘Some things that happen *for the first time... seem* to be happening again... That’s what *déjà vu* is!”

“Just let me write that down, Jackie,” she said, without moving. “I’ll bring it up the next time I want to stop a conversation cold.”

“You can joke about it, but this kind of thing is a desecration of some perfectly fine words. They’re losing their meaning. When people say something was *decimated* they don’t mean ten percent of it was destroyed—they *mean* devastated, so why not *say* devastated?”

“Oh, the horror; the horror,” she said. “How *has* the language survived this long!”

“I could give you another dozen words like that, but how about a great *quote* that people destroy? Liberace said one witty thing in his whole life. Somebody asked him if all the critics who sneered at him made him feel bad, and he said ‘Oh, absolutely—I feel so bad I cry all the way to the bank.' Now people not only don't remember *him,* they ruin his joke by saying 'I *laugh* all the way to the bank'—which doesn't mean *anything*!"

"It's getting late Jackie, and this rain isn't going to let up, so why don't we..."

"People say 'in no way, shape or form,' and that doesn't mean anything, does it? If it can't happen in any *way* then obviously it can't happen in any shape or any form. Have I talked to you about all this before?"

"Jackie," she said, "you've talked to me about *everything* before. At least twice."

"Okay. All right. Point taken. I'll stop."

Their friend Drew Lawrence, who had come in from the street soaking wet, stopped by their table.

"Don't even think about going out there," he said. "It's literally raining cats and dogs!"

Causing Jackie Barron to have the proverbial shit-fit.

Fortunately... not literally.

New York, 1962

Crazy Debbie

Everybody who knew Jackie Barron's friend Debbie Simon knew that she was almost certainly not going to live forever; living through the night often seemed like an uncertain bet.

This was not because she was sickly, because she most certainly wasn't. At 38, it was just that every year of her let-it-all-hang-out life had apparently been the equivalent of a decade in regular-people years.

Three otherwise sane men had been married to her, convinced that *"she'll change when we're married; you'll see,"* which was a perfect example of lust nullifying common sense.

Not that there was anything common about Debbie Simon, not in any sense. Any eager and adventurous young man—or, more often, middle-aged-man pretending not to be a middle-aged man—would immediately recognize and delight in the excitement of encountering a carnally offbeat-beautiful woman who was obviously crazy in a good way.

All of Jackie's friends considered themselves eager and adventurous and longed to be crazy in a good way.

Debbie knew all the places where the night people hung out and—despite being a few years older than most of them—she was welcomed as Queen of the Night. It was, after all, the 60s, and for some New Yorkers—Jackie Barron among them—some form of crazy was required just to seem normal.

Everyone who could tag along looked forward to the occasional late-night visits to the Greek bouzouki clubs that dotted Eighth Avenue. Sometimes Debbie would tear off her blouse—she sometimes neglected to wear a bra—and climb up onto a table, where she would risk dislocating her back, giddy with the pleasure of displaying the moves a belly-dancer had taught her. This broke several laws, along with all the glassware on the table, but usually the owner could be placated by her friends with cash and a promise never to come back. (Except for one club owner, who knew what draws a crowd and *encourage*d her to come back.)

Her current husband, the moderately wealthy and immoderately boring publisher of an insignificant weekly show-biz newspaper, was not one for the night life, so Jackie, drunker but saner, usually assumed responsibility for getting her home. Her husband was always sound asleep when they got there, and, having nothing better to do, Jackie made himself at home on the couch. He was usually still there, sleeping soundly, when the husband left for work in the morning.

Debbie Simon (she had kept her maiden name through all three marriages) was not an all-singing, all-dancing spectacle all the time. While out-drinking any man in the room, she could—and loved to—quote Yeats and Emily Dickinson while she was doing it. On nights when Jackie had a sleepover she would wake him in the morning—or, more likely, early afternoon—with an intimate though innocent kiss.

Debbie was also a writer, and she once created an illustrated book of poems called "Love From A to Z" (*A is for anal/Which dare not speak its name/So forbidding and so welcoming/So anything-but-tame.*). A mimeograph operation on 2nd Street and Avenue B published it in an edition of 50 copies, which sold out immediately. Debbie signed each copy with a lipsticked kiss.

Being awakened between the hours of midnight and three in the morning by a mumbling call from Debbie meant that you were now in the inner-est of her inner-circles. She would explain that she was in the process of suicide, and just calling to say goodbye. The most common reaction to this ritual was, *Oh, for Chrissake; not again. Hold tight; I'm on my way.* So far somebody had always gotten there in time, and she would wind up in Bellevue rather than a cemetery.

Jackie had never been called upon to make that mandatory rite of passage, and when he was, he didn't have to go anywhere. In spite of their better judgment, one particularly overheated August he and Cassandra Sullivan had accepted an invitation to spend a weekend at Debbie's country house. They were peacefully sleeping in the guest room when she crawled up to their bedside and delivered her *cri de coeur*, which came out as "*I'msorryGodI'msorry ... Jus'sorry... Don'tbemad... I'm sorry...*" over and over until Jackie shook her hard and said, "Debbie—what did you take? What?"

He had to repeat that a few times before she waved an unsteady hand back toward her own room and said "I don't know. Everything. Don't be mad. I'm sorry. Don't be mad, Jackie. I'm sorry."

Debbie's current husband was away in Los Angeles, supposedly taking important meetings with newspaper syndicates that never seemed to produce anything, so Jackie unhappily took responsibility for his hostess.

"Yeah, yeah," he said, lifting her up from the floor with his hands under her shoulders. "I know. If you knew how sorry you *look* right now you wouldn't have done this in the first place. Look at me. Look at me!"

Debbie was able to point her face at him, but whether or not she could actually see him was debatable. Her breath was godawful.

"Wake up, Deb. Come on! You know the drill! Tell me what's in your system besides bullshit."

Together they managed to lift her onto the bed they had just vacated, and Cassandra said, "I'll check her room to see if I can find the bottles while you make the call. Remember I told you this 'nice weekend in the country' with Debbie-fucking-Simon was going to turn out bad? Where she's concerned you're as dumb as everybody else. "

"I know, I know, I know," Jackie said, but she was already gone.

The 911 operator couldn't tell him exactly how long it would take for the ambulance to get there, but she definitely told him to keep Debbie awake. Apparently if he let her go to sleep in her condition she might well be on her way to dead.

Keeping her awake was not going to be easy. At least she had already thrown up, and he was grateful for that much.

"Where does she *get* all this stuff?" Cassandra said, offering him the empty bottles of Percocet, Vicodin, Valium and Xanax she had brought back from Debbie's bedroom.

Jackie was busy trying to keep Debbie's eyes open. "She's got lots and lots of really helpful friends," he said.

Debbie was awake enough to know she didn't want to be. "I'll be okay," she said. "I'll be fine. Just take a li'l nap."

"You're not okay, and no naps! Talk to me!" Jackie motioned for Cassandra to help get her on her feet, and together they began walking her.

Debbie decided to be a three-year-old. "Where are we going? I don't want to go anywhere! Tell me a story. Tell me story, Jackie."

"Story. Jesus H. Christ, Debbie! Okay. Okay. Did I ever tell you about the time the guy tried to escape from my uncle's jail?"

"Your uncle's in jail?"

"No; no. My uncle was the Sheriff. He lived downstairs in the jail; the cells were on the second floor."

Debbie's head was nodding as she stumbled along between her rescuers, but she managed to mumble, "Your uncle gonna arres' me? I din' do anything. 'S not my fault, Jackie."

"Nobody's going to arrest you, Debbie. But the Sandman'll eat you alive if you go to sleep. Wake up!"

Debbie's head rocked back and she made an unsuccessful attempt to get Jackie's face into focus. "Talk hillbilly," she said.

"I'll talk any damn kinda talk you wan' me to talk, Deb'ra Jane Simon—"

"It's Deb'ra *Esther* Simon," she said.

"Yeah; yeah; where I come from you'd be Deb'ra Jane. But I'll call you Deberester, it don't make no never-mind to me. I'ma tell you 'bout the jailhouse in Cherokee County, Tennessee, and the prisoner that got buck nekkid and tried to climb out a winder. You listenin' to me?"

"Was he good-lookin', Jackie? I 'on't like stories about ugly."

"Hell, yeah. He was so good-lookin' my aunt near 'bout run off with him! It was her told me this story. My uncle was out catchin' moonshiners when this ol' boy just pushed the bars out of a winder in his cell—nobody ever tried to escape before, so nobody paid much attention to the winders. He put soap all over hisself so's he'd be all slippery, and he started crawlin' out. And you know what happened? You wanna know?"

"I 'on't know," Debbie said. "Do I?"

"You damn well goin' to, because the soap suds didn't work and that good-lookin' ol' boy got stuck in the winder before he could pull his hips through. He couldn' get out and he couldn' get back in. He just started hollerin', and my aunt went up to the cell-floor to see what the hell was goin' on."

Debbie's head was beginning to roll around freely and she was being more dragged than walked. Her eyes were stubbornly shut.

"WAKE UP, dammit! You wanna hear *this* part, Deb, 'cause the first thang my aunt—and my aunt was a good-lookin' woman herself—first thang she saw when she got up to the cells was this ol' boy's bare ass stuck *inside* the winder, with the damndest biggest equipment she ever saw in her life just danglin' there betwixt his legs. He was scareder'n shit, and cryin' and all. Can you get that picture, Deb?"

Cassandra snorted. "She's been *in* a picture like that more times than she's had hot suppers."

Jackie looked at Cassandra, startled. "Where the hell did you learn to say *hot suppers*? Long Island girls don't say *hot suppers.*"

"I reckon I been with you too long, Homer," she said.

"How big was it?" Debbie was still mostly limp, but she was talking a little better and trying—without much success—to support a little of her own weight. "Was it bigger than the sheriff's? Had him and her been fooling around?"

"Ah, Debbie, Debbie. A little sex talk would wake you up in your tomb."

Now her head was rolling again, and her eyes were almost shut.

"Wake up, godammit!" Jackie said. "You want to hear the rest? You want to know what happened? When she reached up and took aholt of that big ol' thang, talkin' to him real soft and all? You wanna know? You wanna hear about what happened when my uncle Isaac walked in on 'em like that?"

Debbie had struggled awake. "No shit?" she said. "The Sheriff caught 'em? Did he shoot 'em both? Did he..."

The doorbell rang and Jackie said, "That's it!" as Cassandra opened the door to the EMT ambulance crew. "No more story. They're here. You're gonna be all right."

After that, Debbie was too busy flirting with the stretcher bearers who were taking her out the door to ask any more questions.

When they were gone, Cassandra sighed deeply, then said, "Well? What *did* happen when your uncle got there?"

"How would I know?" Jackie said, putting his arm around her and leading her back to their bedroom so they could try calling Debbie's husband.

"I was eleven years old, Cassie. My aunt didn't tell me stuff like that."

New York, 1970

Tales Out of School

Jackie Barron knew something was amiss as soon as he heard the somber tone in his friend's voice on the telephone. It was Nick Christoforos, asking if they could meet at McGovern's in about five minutes, to which Jackie responded, as he always did, "Of course."

When Nick was grappling with something that—to him, at least—threatened to spread darkness over the face of the earth, he became very Greek. The corners of his mouth would plunge down toward his jawbone while his eyebrows threatened to collide in the center of his forehead. He felt that his parentage gave him not just a right but a genetic obligation to conjure up deep lines under his haunted eyes in those moments.

Jackie had known Nick for almost twelve years, since they met in the Army in 1958. He was accustomed to these moods, so he recognized a darkness-level of at least seven on a scale of ten as soon as Nick walked in.

"Jesus, Nick; sit down before you melt down," he said.

"Jackie, you have to—"

Jack shushed him with an uplifted hand.

"We need a drink before you tell me when and why the sky is falling," he said.

Eddie the waiter was a middle-aged Irishman who had worked in a taverna in Athens in his youth, and he greeted Nick, as he always did, with "*Yiasou! Ti kanis, Nikos?*"

Nick forced a smile and made the appropriate reply, which Jackie could never quite understand, and they got down to the serious business of ordering. Jackie had a Jack Daniel's on the rocks and Nick just nodded when Eddie said, "Metaxa?" As a favor to Jackie, McGovern kept a bottle of Metaxa behind the bar for Nick, who rarely had more than one.

"The weather's fine, so am I, I don't know any more about how the Mets are doing than you, and I haven't seen or read anything of interest lately, okay? Now—what the hell is *up* with you?"

"It's not me, Jackie—it's Norris."

Norris Carter was a mutual friend who worked very hard at maintaining a playboy image; he had recently stunned them all by announcing that he and Sheila Zanetti—a bright young model professionally called *Sheilo Z*—were engaged.

"Don't tell me the ramblin' rascal has dumped her already," Jackie said. "I'm not surprised but I'm disappointed—Sheila's a terrific girl."

"That's not it, Jackie. What *it* is... I think I have to tell him something that could—probably *will*—destroy the whole relationship."

"What—you found out that she's really a shoe clerk at Macy's, not a semi-super-model?"

"Would you let me talk? This is something only I can do, and I think I have to. Norris is our friend."

"Nikos; Nikos—get a grip. There's just one thing I need to know right now, which is: What the fuck are you talking about?"

Nick finished half the brandy in a single sip and said, "Could I get another one of these?"

"Jesus Christ; this *is* serious."

Jackie caught Eddie's eye and made the universal circular move, meaning bring us another round, ending with his hands clasped prayerfully under his chin, meaning *Now, Eddie; NOW!*

Nick stared into his empty glass until the fresh brandy appeared, finally saying—without looking up—"Remember that party at that guy's house last year?"

"Of course I do," Jackie said. "His name was Sal Fialla and he and Sheila went to high school together. He'd invited a bunch of the old crowd for a reunion, and Sheila invited Norris and me and you so she could have somebody from her grown-up life there."

He shook his head in unwelcome memory. "I'm sure I've been that bored *some* other evening in my life," he said, "but I'm damned if I can remember when it could have been. Thank God for Jack Daniel's."

"Okay; here's the thing," Nick said. "I called Fialla a few days later to see if I left my gloves at his house, and... he told me something."

Jackie abided the silence for a moment before saying, "And?"

"And he told me... he told me he walked into a little back room he keeps for storage, looking for another Chianti that night. And Sheila was there. She was sitting down with her skirt up around her waist and there was a guy on his knees on the floor in front of her, and... you know."

"No, Nick, I don't *know*. But I'm probably guessing right."

"Sal couldn't see who it was because—God, I hate this!—because the guy's head was buried under her skirt. Sal says he left fast; he's not sure she even saw him. It wasn't so much that he was shocked. More disappointed. When he asked the other guys later, nobody took the blame. Or credit, I guess.

"Now the bad part. He said it was just like high school days, Jackie. Said Sheila was a good Catholic girl in those days, determined to stay a virgin. But the guys on the football team or in the Honor Society all knew she'd do anything *but*."

Jackie took a certain pride in being unshockable himself, so he recuperated quickly.

"Let's not get carried away, Nick. She and Norris were just casually dating at Sal's party; she wasn't *cheating*. Not exactly. If it was a *guy* getting swept away like that at a party, you'd have said *Attaboy!* and listened to him brag afterwards."

"Come on, Jackie; you know this is different. I've kept the secret, and I always would've—I don't pass judgment—but—*Norris is marrying her*! If she was *doing* every guy in high school, and being *done* by that guy that night... who else is doing her now? Norris has a right to know, Jackie. And I'm the one who's got to tell him."

Jackie disagreed, and he argued the point until Nick turned down a third Metaxa and said he had to go, meaning his mind was made up.

They walked to the door together, with Jackie insisting that "telling the whole truth isn't all it's cracked up to be, you know." Nick wasn't buying it.

When they got to the sidewalk Jackie gave up and went back inside, taking out his phone book on his way to the back of the bar.

A woman's voice answered when he dialed, and he said, "Sheila, it's Jackie. Jackie. Barron. Uh... fine, thanks. Listen... remember that party at Sal Fialla's?

"Well... we may have a problem."

Los Angeles, 1967

Wait'll Lenny Bruce Hears About *This*

A rubber trash barrel crunched under his right front wheel and Jackie Barron rcalized he had driven up over the curb while he was pulling out of the parking place.

At two o'clock in the morning on a deserted residential block it didn't seem important to stop, so he didn't. Not until a siren behind him made a brief burping sound and a revolving red light illuminated the street.

No problem, he thought. *I'm cool. No harm done. I can handle this. No big deal.*

Jackie had been drinking on Sunset Boulevard for a while. An hour or so. Maybe more. *This is Frank Zappa's fault,* he thought. *If The Mothers hadn't been playing I wouldn't have gone into that bar. Fucking Frank Zappa!*

He hoped the Johnnie Walker Black (rocks; water-back) wouldn't be as strong on his breath as it was in his mouth.

The officer who asked Jackie for license and registration was tall and broad. Not fat, just broad; there were no fat people in the revamped, 1960s L.A. Police Department. The officer could have been a linebacker for the L.A. Rams.

Lenny Bruce calls them 'peace officers,' not cops. 'Peace officers.' Everything's cool.

Jackie had left the top down on the rented 1967 Thunderbird convertible. The other officer, after checking out the back seat, pulled the linebacker aside for a whispered conference.

When the first office came back—he was apparently the senior man—he leaned into the car, eye-to-eye with Jackie. He didn't look peaceful. Everything wasn't cool.

"Step out of the car, Jonathan," he said.

Jonathan? Jesus Christ. Nobody's called me 'Jonathan' since... ever. This is not good. Not good at all.

"Where'd you get the wallet, Jonathan?"

The question made no sense and Jackie struggled for an answer. "Uh ... it's mine," he said, offering it to the officer. "It's got my union card, all that stuff. You can..."

Jackie was standing next to the car now, and the linebacker-cop didn't break eye contact when he delivered a short, sharp blow to the stomach. Jackie didn't scream. He just said "*Hunh*!" and tried to get his breath back.

Whoa. Whoa. This is a mistake. This is—

"Don't get cute with us, Jonathan," the linebacker said softly, pushing Jackie's wallet aside. "We really hate it when people get cute with us. You know what wallet I mean."

Why does he care where I got my wallet? Jackie thought. *I have no idea where I got it*. The question made no sense, but at least he wasn't asking about drinking, and that was good.

"That's the only wallet I've got," he said. "I've had it a long time."

"That the best you can do?" the officer said.

The next punch was as unexpected as the first. Jackie made the "*Hunh*!!" sound again, thinking *Wrong guy! Can't he see I'm the wrong guy?*

"Didn't I see you throwing stuff at us in those anti-war riots last month?" the linebacker said. "You guys embarrass President Johnson, you call us pigs and lie about it, and then you steal wallets to pay your bail; is that how it goes?"

"Wait! Please. Wait," Jackie said, gasping now. "Wasn't me. I don't even live here. Came in from New York. Yesterday. I work for IBN. Television. Really. ID's in the wallet. In *my* wallet, I mean. *My* wallet!"

"I don't care if you work for Walter Cronkite," the linebacker said. "I'll arrest him, too, if I catch him making trouble on my watch."

The next punch was on the other side, but still in the softness of Jackie's belly.

Not happening, he thought. *People don't hit me. Doesn't he know that?*

"Swear to God. Officer. I swear to God. Not me," he said.

"Know how I can tell when a New York guy is lying, Jonathan? His lips are moving."

He'll be embarrassed when he realizes he's got the wrong man, Jackie thought. *He'll probably apologize. Turn back into a peace officer.*

The other officer had come back from the prowl car.

"You seem a little short-winded, Jonathan," the linebacker said. "Probably smoke too much. You just turn around and put both hands on the car. You can stand there and think about it for a minute."

Leaning on the car while the two uniforms whispered, Jackie guessed at a probable scenario. Someone probably stole a wallet in this neighborhood. Probably emptied it and threw it into the open convertible.

Goddamn. Why didn't I put the top up, Jackie thought. *Wrong place, wrong time. These guys don't trust anybody under thirty. Goddammit; I'm not under thirty! This isn't right!* As breathing became a little easier, Jackie became a little calmer. Even optimistic. *Maybe the other cop found out I'm not who they want,* he thought. *Maybe they'll just apologize and send me on my way. They don't even have to apologize.*

Trying to piece his mind back together, Jackie concentrated on the other cop. *He's not a linebacker* he thought. *More a beach-boy. Maybe even a Beach Boy. Help me, Rhonda, help help me Rhonda. Please.*

When they came back they came with a Breathalyzer.

"How's it goin'?" Jackie said to the beach-boy, feeling idiotic even before the words were out of his mouth. "I think your partner got a little over-excited."

"Shutting up would be a really good idea for you right now, Jonathan," the linebacker said amiably. "I believe you've had a few tonight, haven't you?"

"I had a couple... it's Saturday night. Hasn't everybody had a couple?" The officer was not amused.

Jackie tried again: "You found the wallet-guy, huh?" he said.

"Don't worry about that," the linebacker said. "Just put this in your mouth and take a deep breath."

"Aren't you going to—"

The linebacker took Jackie's jaw in his hand, but not roughly. "Mouth," he said. "Deep breath."

Jackie did as he was told, and the linebacker was grinning when he showed the beach-boy the results.

"I think we have to get you off the streets, Jonathan," he said. "You're too drunk to *walk*, never mind drive. You're a moving violation just standing there. Turn around, please."

With his hands cuffed behind his back, and the linebacker's hand on the top of his head, Jackie bent low and stumbled getting into the back of the prowl car.

"So... uh... you gonna tell me what happened?" he asked when he was seated.

"Nothing happened," the linebacker-officer said, not bothering to turn and look at him. "You're drunk, you were driving, you're under arrest. That's all you need to know."

"Well," Jackie said, "I bet you're sorry you hit me now, aren't you?"

This time the linebacker cop *did* turn. He reached back over the seat to take a handful of Jackie's shirt at the collar. "What do you mean, Jonathan? Nobody *hit* you. That kinda lie won't work; don't even try it. You people got to learn there are *consequences* to your actions." He tightened the grip on Jackie's shirt. "You wouldn't make a *stupid* mistake like that, would you?"

Sitting in handcuffs in the middle of the night in a neighborhood with no witnesses walking by, Jackie was not interested in making stupid mistakes of any kind.

"No, no," he said. "I was kidding. Whatever you say. It's over. Never happened."

He didn't talk any more after that. *I know I failed that drunk test*, he thought. *Who's gonna believe some straight-arrow LA cop pounded my belly? Even I wouldn't believe me.*

Tonight's lesson: Next time I read about some sadass loser who claims he ran because he was scared of the police—I'll think twice before I doubt him. They do this to a middle-class white guy with a steady job... 1967 Thunderbird convertible—a RED Thunderbird convertible for God's sake!... what happens to a South LA Mexican kid in a chopped and channeled '52 Chevy? His body was relaxing, and he almost laughed.

Jackie thought of Jack Webb on "Dragnet" saying "Take him downtown and book him." He thought of Johnny Cash singing about Folsom Prison.

I'm going to spend a night in jail. That's what Hemingway would do, he thought. *It's okay. First offense. I'll sleep it off, I'll pay a fine and go home in the morning. I can live with that.*

And if he ever met Lenny Bruce, now they could discuss this subject as equals.

Los Angeles, 1967

Doing Hard Time

Jackie Barron had been in jail for half his life, or at least twelve hours.

Doesn't matter, he thought. Twelve hours or sixteen years. Doesn't matter. They're never going to let me out. They forgot I'm here. I'm not supposed to be here. They forgot. Judge said I could go. Three hours ago he said that. Why am I still here?

Jackie looked around, careful not to make eye contact with anyone. The holding cell was only slightly larger than his very small living room. Yeah, he thought, my living room. Dying room? I had thirty-six people in my living room at a party once. I think it was thirty-six. Yeah. Thirty-six. How many people in here? Probably two or three people besides me. The rest are troglodytes. Troglodytes and demons and child-killers. I bet there's a hundred. More. And I don't know any of them. Please God, don't let me meet any of them.

The troglodyte, if such he be, standing closest to Jackie was not only someone he did not want to meet; he was someone Jackie would have prayed never to even see outside of a movie. His jaw was bigger than Jackie's chest. There weren't any arms on his tee-shirt, and his own arms would have ripped the seams even if they'd been there. Thank God he wasn't staring at Jackie. Thank God he looked too hung-over to stare at anything more than an inch or two beyond his own bulging eyes. Unfortunately, there seemed to be many of his bloodline in this celled population.

Jackie had two overwhelming fears that stuck in his throat like fists. The judge had fined him $250 for drunk driving and turned him loose three hours ago. But then the cop said, "Oh, no—you came in at 2 o'clock this morning. There wasn't anybody around to take your picture and book you. You'll just wait in here a few minutes and then we'll take care of all that."

Slam. A few minutes. Three hours ago. Other guys got called out of the holding cell and went away, but Jackie didn't. Jackie stood because there wasn't anyplace to sit down except for the benches where some mean-looking men already sat, and when one of these men got up to leave Jackie didn't hurry over to take that seat on the bench. It didn't seem like a good idea. If he was going to be here until he died, he would at least die standing up like a man.

They sent my release papers to the wrong place, Jackie thought. Like in the Army. If you hated a Sergeant and he was going to Japan you accidentally sent his pay-records to Germany. Fucked him up for months. Those cops who took turns hitting me last night—only in the stomach, no marks—those cops probably hate me. I didn't tell on them; why would they hate me? Doesn't matter. They sent my release from the judge to Germany. I'll be fucked up for months. Maybe literally.

I don't have a dime to use the damn pay phone. Nobody knows I'm here. I could have made my one call from the police station last night. I didn't want to call anybody. It would be cool to spend a night in jail. Like Hemingway or somebody. What kind of fucking fool am I? It wasn't cool. At least it wasn't perdition. This is perdition.

Jackie's other fear was that he wouldn't die but would vomit on some giant anal-rape-murderer standing next to him and be forced to eat his own genitals. Jackie didn't want to die of old age in a holding cell in the Los Angeles City jail, but choking to death on his own genitals would probably be even worse.

The prisoner who was looking at him quizzically and pushing his way through the crowd towards him didn't look like a rape-murderer. He was probably twenty years old—a kid, at least ten years younger than Jackie—with a little blonde stubble that barely showed on his cheeks. He didn't look like one of the mean guys. Road-weary and probably older than he ought to be, but not mean.

"Hang on, Sloopy," the boy said softly when he reached Jackie.

"What? What did you say?"

The boy shrugged. "It's just a song. The McCoys. Big hit last year. You standing there looking like you might forget to breathe just reminded me of that title, that's all. You just need to hang on. I'm gonna guess you never been anywhere like this before, am I right?"

Jackie wasn't forgetting to breathe, he was just having a difficult time doing it. His eyes cut around the room, wondering if anyone was noticing this. If he talked to this kid would the bad guys think he was a fairy and beat them both up?

"No. I never been. And I'm not supposed to be now. There's been some kinda mistake."

The boy grinned. "Yeah, I know. Every poor sumbitch in here isn't supposed to be here. We're all not guilty. It's just a big mistake."

"That's not what I meant," Jackie said. He noticed that he didn't have much voice, and it seemed to come from the roof of his mouth. "I'm guilty. I was pulling away from the curb when they stopped me. They thought I stole a wallet. I didn't, but they'd already beat me up before they found that out. Didn't matter. I flunked the breath test. I was guilty of that. The public defender this morning said I flunked it worse than anybody he'd ever seen. I think he was impressed. But I'm not a real criminal. Really. I just want to get my picture taken and go home. Am I talking too fast? Yeah. I am. Too fast and too much. I'm sorry."

The boy was grinning, but softly. "No," he said. "That's normal. It takes a while to get used to the process. You're just caught in the process, that's all. They'll have you out of here pretty soon."

Jackie was breathing easier. The boy didn't seem to mean him any harm. "How come you're so cool? You're stuck here, too."

"I'm used to it," the boy said. "Believe me, this ain't the worst jail you could be in. You should try the jail in Winslow, Arizona. Meanest people and the nastiest jail on earth. Not that I been in every jail on earth. But my share."

"Am I allowed to ask what you're in for?"

"What I'm in here for doesn't matter. You're the one looking like you been sentenced to hang at sundown. Do your people know where you are?"

Jackie snorted. "No. They took away my money and everything else when they arrested me. I'd have to have a dime for that phone. Where'm I gonna get a dime?" Jackie's hands were clenched. Like his teeth. He felt like his hair was clenched.

The boy shrugged and reached in his pocket. "From me," he said. "I been in The System here since Friday night. They let you have some of your stuff back on the third day." He looked at the coins in his hand. There were some pennies, a nickel and one dime. "Here," he said. "Call somebody."

Jackie couldn't believe what was happening. "Wait a minute," he said. "What about you? You've only got one dime."

The boy took the coin and tapped on Jackie's hand until he opened it. "What'm I gonna do with a dime?" he said. "There's nobody closer than Austin who cares where I am, and a dime won't call Austin. I'm gonna be around for a while. Hanging paper and running up credit cards won't get me the death penalty, but with my record—and that interstate stuff—I'mo be around for a while. Make your damn call."

"Thank you," Jackie said. "Thank you! I'll just be a minute. I'll call my friends so they'll know I'm okay." He heard himself and stopped. "Not that I'm okay," he said. "Nothing's okay. But you're an okay guy. And I'm gonna leave you some money as soon as I collect my stuff. Write down your name—or just tell it to me—and I won't forget. Jesus; I can't believe you're doing this. I can't believe a dime for a phone call is saving my life. But I'll tell you this—I'll tell you this—if they come after me again—they'll never take me alive."

It was Jackie's turn to grin for the first time in—well, it felt like the first time in his life. The first time in this life, anyway.

"I made a joke," he said. "I'm just a convicted drunk but I'm talking like a black & white gangster movie. Can you believe I made a *joke*?"

The boy punched him lightly, playfully on the shoulder. "See? You're gonna be all right. Once you've made your first joke it's all easy-time from there on."

Jackie took his first deep breath. Maybe he'd survive this half of his life, too.

New York, 1974

No Fault, No Foul

Patricia Mackenzie was in the process of getting fired for being beautiful when Jackie Barron walked onto the set.

It was her first job since she'd made history as the only female still-photographer in the New York union. It was also her second day of shooting on a new IBN television series starring Martin DeFranco.

The Indie Broadcasting Network, feeling a little pressure from the women's movement in the changing times of 1974, had been eager to hire her. She was a well-regarded freelance, and the hiring—even just for this one series—raised the Publicity Department's total number of women with creative assignments, finally, to... one.

Jackie would be the network publicist on the series; he knew her slightly and he was happy because he had seen her work and liked the look of it. He was also happy because he'd seen Patricia Mackenzie, and he liked the look of *her*, too.

She had started work on the series the day before Jackie did, and all her bright professional prospects were turning to rust and recriminations by the time he arrived on the set.

As soon as the blinking red light on the door was turned off, allowing him to come in, Jackie was grabbed by the series producer, who said, "It's about time you got here. What the *hell* are we going to do about your photographer?"

This was not something Jackie wanted to hear. Ever.

"Oh, God," he said. "Already? What's she done?"

"Nothing she shouldn't be doing," the producer said. "She's a dream; everywhere at once, floats like a cloud, just the way you said she would. But it doesn't matter. The bitch is complaining about everything, and she's glared shitballs at the pretty photographer from the minute she walked in. Something's going to blow."

"Patricia's offended DeFranco?"

"No—she's offended *Mrs.* DeFranco by being gorgeous on the same set as her husband."

DeFranco had been a big star, singing the songs of Cole Porter and George Gershwin and acting in movies. When the '50s ended, so did his career. Rock 'n' roll turned him into a nostalgia question, and playing a private eye in this series was his best shot at making a comeback while there was still something to come back to.

Before he married Richenda Courtney he'd been known as "Party-Hearty Marty" in Vegas, and she was becoming notorious for watching him like a prison guard.

Jackie was not a happy man. Finding Patricia Mackenzie sitting on the floor in an empty corner of the studio, cleaning a camera and scowling, did not change that.

"What seems to be the trouble here, ma'am?" he asked rhetorically.

"Fuck you," she answered softly.

"That bad, is it?"

"The woman is crazy. She thinks it's still the '50s and I'm making a pass at DeFranco's skinny ass."

The producer joined them, looking anxious, determined, and miserable all at once.

"I got to talk to both of you," he said. "Patricia, you're doing a helluva job, *helluva* job, but my hands are tied. Courtney called somebody in Programming and the call crawled up the ladder to the head of the network. Final word is, she wins."

Patricia was in no mood to be diplomatic. "Who's running the show here," she said, "you or her?"

"Believe me, sweetheart, it ain't me," the producer said. "The bitch-wife has DeFranco so buffaloed he can't go to the toilet by himself. I'm *really* sorry about this, but I need you to pack up and go."

Jackie went back to the network with her that afternoon, and tried to look supportive while she yelled at the VP of Public Relations. The VP agreed that she got a lousy deal, promised her fair payment and more work in the future, and sent her home anyway. Jackie spoke up on her behalf, but the VP said, "I know she's not to blame, Jackie. And I know it doesn't make any difference. We'll do better for you on the next one, Patricia."

As it turned out, there wasn't any next one.

IBN sent her a check for two weeks work which she sent back. Patricia was mad. There was a principle involved, and she filed a sexual discrimination lawsuit.

Jackie, who had established a casual relationship with her, applauded the move and prayed he would not be called upon to testify on her behalf. His network bosses would most certainly consider such a display of gallantry as probable cause for his dismissal, too.

She eventually took a sizeable settlement from IBN, but that was the end of Patricia Mackenzie with all the networks. She had become unfortunately famous as *that-girl-who-sues-people.*

Jackie would occasionally run into her on a set, shooting for some magazine or other. Usually they would have lunch together when that happened, and sometimes when it didn't. Patricia was recently divorced but Jackie wasn't yet, so mostly they made small talk about which famous people they'd been working with; who was nice and who was a colossal pain in the ass.

They avoided any hint of romance until two years later, when Jackie's wife left him. He waited a respectful few weeks and then he called Patricia. After that they stopped avoiding anything.

Turned out they were very compatible, and neither was interested in keeping secrets. Jackie told Patricia all about his failed marriage. When his wife figured out that he just didn't much like being married she decided enough was more than enough. The ending was angry but not murderous.

In Patricia's case, it had been the husband who wanted a divorce.

"He was a lawyer and he fell for a client," she said. "One time he actually said she was sexier than me. To my face. I signed the divorce papers, considered suicide for about eight seconds, and then I decided just to fuck all his friends. And several guys he hated. I made them all wonder how he could have been crazy enough to leave such a treasure. I finally came to my senses one night when I was at a party and realized I'd slept with every man in the room."

"Patricia," Jackie said, "your husband is so full of shit he gurgles. I can personally testify that if you were any sexier you'd be illegal in 36 states."

They had their share of differences, but they all seemed to be manageable.

He had no interest in the ballet, or in traveling to Brooklyn, but he went to the Brooklyn Academy with her to see some Russian troupe.

She missed the beard he'd worn when they met, so he grew it back.

She didn't write him off as a lost cause when he insisted that Bernard Shaw was a more important writer than Shakespeare.

Her idea of fashion wasn't Victoria's Secret, but she built up a separate, at-home wardrobe for special occasions. By mutual agreement, these occasions occurred almost as often as ordinary occasions.

He explained to her his belief about mouths. "All that stuff about the eyes being the window of the soul is just a well-meaning myth. Some poet made it up to prove he was sensitive. The lips are the window—and the entryway—to the soul, and everything else. I'm always watching your lips. If you catch me looking into your eyes, I'm probably up to something."

"Give it up, Jackie," she said. "Depending on your mood you're just as likely to say my ass is the window to the soul."

"No, your lips are where I saw the real you. They're what I loved about you first. The rest followed, of course. Your bottom is gorgeous, and so are your eyes and your...

uh... reproductive organs. But your lips, Pattymac; your lips!"

She let it drop. But she did take a moment to suggest that watching lips might just mean he was hard of hearing.

After a few months Patricia confronted him with her first real complaint.

"You've never said you love me, Jackie. That's a lie of omission. *You love me*! You know you do."

She was right, and Jackie had no difficulty in saying so, then and from then on. He just hadn't gotten around to saying it before.

After that, things settled into a wonderfully untroubled rhythm, until the night he arrived at her front door and found her waiting with an uncharacteristically somber face.

She said: "Sit down. We have to talk."

That was in 1978. Jackie was already 43 years old, which was old enough to know that nothing good ever begins *we have to talk.*

It wasn't just the words. It was her tone of voice. Not angry, not accusatory. More like affection sautéed in melancholy.

He sat.

She got right to the point. "You're never going to marry again, are you?"

They had talked about a lot of things in their year together, but marriage wasn't one of them. Still, it wasn't a subject he'd never thought about on his own.

"Probably not," he said. "I won't say it can't happen. I never thought I'd marry in the first place, but I did. Best I can say is... it's not something I would look forward to."

"That's what I thought. And that's okay. I may not marry again either. But I don't like to think that door's shut. The difference is this: to you, not being married means freedom. To me, having the *choice* about being married is freedom. If I feel that deeply about someone—and I definitely intend for that to keep happening—I want to know there's someplace for it to go. Being with you has been..."

The sound of *has been*—past tense—rang of a eulogy. Jackie started preparing himself for the next clod to fall.

"It's been wonderful, but I think it has to be over."

His memory of the rest of the conversation was never too precise. At the end of the evening they agreed that their decision to end the relationship was sad but not ugly.

They went to bed and made love, and there was melancholy in the lovemaking. The next morning he gathered up the clothes he kept in her closet. He held on to her key so he could feed her cat when she was away on assignment.

They had the occasional dinner together. They took vacations in Rhode Island and in Maine. They always took a single room and slept together.

Literally. Slept. When the romance ended, the sex, by unspoken agreement, did too. Jackie, of course, insisted that she never tell anyone that they *only* slept together on these trips. ("Bad for my reputation.") The friendship was affectionate, but the concept of friends with benefits hadn't yet come into currency.

Jackie helped her load the car when she left to begin a new life in North Carolina. When she was seated behind the wheel he leaned in through the window and kissed her.

"We're unique in my life," he said. "We're a *Nobody Done Nobody Wrong Song*. No tears, no recriminations. Well... maybe a tear."

Patricia smiled softly and said, "You're right. On both counts. And it was great while it lasted."

Jackie smiled and sighed. "As usual, we're in agreement."

"Of course," she said. "And we owe it all to Richenda Courtney."

Resurrection College, 1944

Boys Will be Boys

The boy was dangling upside down with his legs mostly in the room but the rest of him flattened up against the outside wall, with nothing to hang onto. He was draped like a banner from the second-story window of a summer-camp dorm at Resurrection College.

He was not hanging there because it was fun. He didn't seem to be having any fun at all.

He was doing it because he didn't have any choice. He was an unimpressive nine-year-old, and the twelve-year-old with the shock of dirty blonde hair and the permanent sneer had pulled the boy's pants down and tipped him backwards through the window.

The twelve-year-old definitely thought it was fun. He was holding onto the boy's ankles, and his weight was the only thing holding his victim in place. He was also leaning out the window himself so he could look down at the terrified face and say, "Hey, little jackoff, you havin' fun? We're havin' fun. How come you're not? I heard you liked it with your pants down. Why don't you reach up there and get aholt of yourself? Huh? I bet you'd be having fun then!"

The twelve-year-old's name was Billy Gentry, and he laughed and whooped when he finished asking this. The three boys who stood at the window, sharing the laugh, were all younger than him. Younger, but not so obviously weak as Eddie Johnson, which was the nine-year-old's name.

Jackie Barron, at age eleven, stood respectfully behind the jeering group. He was not with Billy Gentry's little band of bullies, but—being not only younger but not much more than half Billy's size—he darn well knew not to be against them, either. He felt bad for the even-smaller boy hanging out the window, but he didn't want to join him.

Jackie was used to most boys being bigger than him, so what he always did—usually with some success—was single out the biggest, toughest kids around and try to make them laugh. He had managed this pretty well at home in Hutchins, Tennessee, but he was still feeling his way in the treacherous territory that was Summer Bible Camp.

He decided to take a chance.

"You know what you really ought to do, Billy?" he said. "You ought to get that big dumb pig Mr. Jackass-son hanging up here by his heels with his drawers off, like the oink-oink he is!"

Mr. Jackson was the Camp Counselor who put them through the torture of pushups and deep knee bends every morning before breakfast. Billy Gentry hated the councilor, and there was a good chance that Jackie calling him "Mr. Jackass-son" would get the bully's attention. Imagining this ex-Marine Phys Ed teacher hanging by his heels with his pants down was pretty sure to get a laugh from Billy and his friends.

It did.

"That's a good idea!" Billy said, turning his head to look at Jackie with approval. "Dudden nobody deserve it more."

"You'd prob'ly have to go up to the third floor to hang him out to dry," Jackie said. 'If you hung him from here his pumpkin head would drag on the ground and get snot all over the place."

That got a roar. Saying "snot" or "fart" was guaranteed to get a laugh anytime, anywhere.

"Maybe he'll be next to get what's comin' to him!" Billy said.

"What did this little twerp do, anyway?" Jackie asked.

"I don't like him, idden that enough? Besides which, I heard he was playin' with hisself in his bed last night," Billy said. "That's disgusting! Looks to me like he ain't but about five years old, anyways. Idden that what he looks like to you?"

"Naw; I don't think a five-year-old would know *how* to play with himself," Jackie said. "I bet he's at least *six*. But that might not make any difference. Shoot, I bet he can't even *find* his little pecker!"

It was working. Everybody was looking at Jackie and grinning now. The next part would be the tricky part.

"Why don't you just go ahead and drop him," he said. "I still got some of my allowance left; we can go over to the campus store and I'll buy us some Co-Colas to celebrate."

Jackie knew there was no real danger that Eddie would be dropped. Billy Gentry was dumb but he wasn't stupid.

"Well, I been thinkin' about droppin' him," Billy said, "but if I did, my daddy would just get mad at me all over again. This little jerkoff ain't worth it."

Jackie let out the breath he'd been holding. He had seen Billy Gentry with his parents when they arrived, and heard Billy's daddy say, "You get in some kinda damn trouble again, I swear I'll tear off your leg and beat you with the bloody stump!" It was only fair that Billy had somebody that scared the pee-pee out of him, too.

The idea of some Co-Colas sounded good, and the fun was wearing off a little anyway. Eddie Johnson got pulled back in through the window and dropped on the floor. He just lay there, shaking and looking at his tormentors.

"Aw, don't be *cryin'* all over the place," Billy said. "Ain't nobody hurt you. Just keep your hands off that little thang between your legs from now on or I'll cut it off for you, you understand?"

Eddie Johnson didn't actually know what Billy was talking about, but he nodded his head in frantic agreement.

"I better help the little baby up or he'll still be here sniveling at breakfast time tomorrow," Jackie said. "I heard Mr. Jackass-son plays with himself all the time, so he'd prob'ly take this pud-puller home with him."

This got the hoped-for laugh, and Jackie knelt down to take the smaller boy under the arms, leaning his face in close to Eddie's ear.

"Just keep your mouth shut and keep lookin' scared," he whispered. "And don't you dare tell anybody about this or these boys'll make you wish you never been born. And me, too."

Standing up, Jackie said aloud, "I hope you learned your lesson here. Next time you want to play with yourself, go ask Mr. Jackass-son to help you!"

With his back to the other boys, Jackie winked at Eddie Johnson.

New York, 1984

Old Army Buddies

On a typical morning in 1958 Pvt. Jackie Barron was stationed unhappily at Fort Dix, New Jersey. He was gearing down for another long and boring day clerking in the Personnel office when Pvt. John-Paul Goodson made his spectacular entrance.

The new clerk had the cuffs of his khaki uniform tucked into the top of his boots, his shirt had been tailored to fit his body in a way that the Army quartermaster had never intended, and his cap sat at a cocky angle almost touching his right eyebrow. Instead of the regulation black tie, he wore a black scarf knotted around his throat. John-Paul Goodson cut a dashing figure.

The Sergeant who ran the office did not approve of dashing figures. While Jackie and the other clerks pretended not to stare, the Sergeant barked.

"What the HELL are you supposed to be, trooper? You're goddamn out of uniform!"

Pvt. Goodson looked at him innocently. "I was told to report in dress khakis," he said. "I can go back and change into fatigues if that's not right."

The Sergeant was not amused. He stood glowering while the newcomer pulled his cuffs out of the boots, took off his cap and smoothed down his hair, which was slightly longer than the military approved. He was lectured: No boots with the dress uniform. A real tie; GI issue. Cap straight on the head, not tipped in any direction.

"And get rid of about half that hair before you come in here tomorrow!"

John-Paul agreed so graciously that he obviously felt he was doing the Sergeant a favor, and Jackie Barron felt sure he was about to make a friend.

In 1984 Jackie had been back in New York for 24 years; no longer a soldier, no longer a clerk, and walking reluctantly through the front door of St. Vincent's Hospital. He hated hospital visits, but he had a personal rule: When an old friend has been there for more than two weeks—that's serious. You visit. Especially if the old friend is former-Private John-Paul Goodson.

It was hard to understand how—and why—this very unmilitary soldier had gotten past the Draft Board—even in peacetime. It was also pretty near impossible to imagine him surviving Basic Training without being beaten to death by the mixed-bag of macho young draftees.

He explained his survival as, "a miracle of masquerade. For those eight weeks I was straighter than John Wayne."

John-Paul's new, East Coast, city-bred comrades-in-arms simply shrugged, shook their heads and said, "*what a character*!" The few small-town boys in the unit, some of whom had never met a Jew, a Catholic, or a homosexual, weren't sure quite what to make of him. Still, his craftily composed disdain for the Regular Army sergeants around them personified everyone's silent battle-cry of "FTA!" meaning "*Fuck The Army*." They admired him for that.

Jackie and the other New Yorkers in the barracks were pretty sure about what to make of him, and John-Paul was delighted to find a few fellow peacetime-warriors who, even though handicapped by being straight, knew the entire scores to Broadway musicals.

The pale green walls made the hospital corridors as dreary as a serious place presumably should be. The plastic-wrapped meals on the passing lunch carts looked to be plastic themselves.

The halls were populated by green-gowned patients, some pulling intricate carts that slowly dripped something into a vein, some joking with the nurses as they were pushed along in wheelchairs.

Others were too skeletal to stand, their faces too haunted by fear and helplessness for joking. John-Paul had never shown either fear or helplessness, and—no matter how ill he might be—it was unlikely he had succumbed to either.

Jackie and Nick Christoforos had created a theater in Service Club One at Fort Dix, and they welcomed the newcomer into their circle. He told them he had been a fashion designer "back in the real world." A boy-wonder at 22. With the least provocation he would whip out a review of his 1957 Fashion Week showing. Jackie took the clipping and read the conclusion aloud. "It says here, 'The talented Jean-Paul Goodson has reached full fruition at a shockingly early age with his stunning new line.'"

"A meaningless observation," John-Paul said. "I'd been fully fruited for years."

He explained that, *professionally*, he was *Jean-Paul*—pronounced with as fine a faux French accent as he could muster. Over his objections, the Army had insisted on registering him as the more mundane "John-Paul," although he was allowed to keep the hyphen. Not that it made much difference; in the military nobody was ever called by his first name.

He never thought of his friendship with straight guys as evidence of their noble tolerance. "You try *tolerating* me for one minute," he once said to a group he was drinking with, "and I'll show you how quickly the Enchanted Fairy can turn into The Wicked Witch.

"Mind you, I don't think I'm better than you," he continued, "but I do think *I'm* the one being tolerant. There's not a one of you who can even pronounce *haute couture*. Everyone who knows what *haute couture* is, raise your hand. Oh, never mind. You know who you aren't.

"I also don't think I'm better than you big-butch-mannabees simply because I was living with a genuine English Lady of an uncertain age when I got drafted."

As often happened, his companions weren't sure they believed anything he said, but he could usually be counted on for a colorful, if questionable, story.

"I was working at Bergdorf's when I met her. I told her why the dress she was about to buy would look ridiculous on her. Then I showed her the *fabulous* one that God *meant* for her to wear—which cost more than we'll make in our whole two years here—and she took a shine to me. Trust me; I *shone* in those days. She wrapped me up, took me home to her simple eight-room apartment on Fifth Avenue, and gradually turned me into the breathtaking fashion-designer I was always meant to be."

He pushed up the left sleeve of his sky-blue cashmere sweater, displaying a Rolex watch. Most of them had never seen a Rolex watch, but he told them what it cost, so they admired it.

"Trust me, my darlings, this is *not* a Chinatown rip-off. Lady Sylvia's proper English eccentricities included an unlikely passion for country music and elegant faggots. I fit that last requirement right down to my Gucci loafers. Which she also paid for."

John-Paul Goodson might have been from a separate planet, but who cared? True or false, his outrageous tales lightened the atmosphere in the Army-drab barracks.

"I've known some extraordinary people," he said. "The Duchess had been keeping me for a year. She cried like an ingénue when I told her I wasn't going to announce myself as a queer just to stay out of the Army. Spending two years saluting old men wearing gold bars was a lot safer than opening myself to all those nasty laws that make me a leper. Just look around you, my darlings—you damn well know that many of your brothers-in-arms are sisters at heart. The Army is perfectly willing to look the other way so long as we don't do it in the streets and frighten the Drill Sergeants.

"Still," he said. "I'm a flamingo, and a beige flamingo is just plain unnatural." He laughed. "Not that I ever minded being unnatural. Just not in khaki."

Every day at Fort Dix was a challenge for Pvt. John-Paul, as he looked, always, for ways to be just flamboyant enough to satisfy himself without facing a court-martial. There was no such thing as Chinese food in the Mess Hall but he sometimes brought chopsticks to eat with. In the barracks he often wore an ankle-length silk kimono. On winter weekends the faint fragrance of Joy perfume was always there, sprinkled on his Italian-imported sweaters.

In the two years they all served, he was never promoted to Private First Class. He never expected to be.

After wandering the halls for a while Jackie finally found the number they had given him. It was a private room, which made him smile. Didn't matter what it cost; John-Paul would find a way to have a room where he could hold court.

Jackie and his friends sometimes called him "John-Paul-Peacock," because he loved to goad them with stories about the cruising-bars with blacked-out windows on Columbus Avenue in New York. They were called "the bird circuit" because they had names like The Blue Cockatoo, The Pink Flamingo and The Jackdaw Lounge.

When he got the evil glint in his eye and began to describe the ritual cruising that went on in these bars, or the brutal arrogance of leather-queens in the S&M bars, somebody—usually Nick Christoforos—would say something like "Oh, for God's sake, John-Paul! You're talking about '*the love that dare not speak its name.*' So will you please just *shut up* about it! If you tell me that you went to those S&M bars even once I'll go straight to Sgt. Rivera and kick your closet open!"

"Too late, Nickie. I was out of the closet at ten."

By 1984 pretty much everyone—with the apparent exception of Ronald Reagan—knew about AIDS. Jackie was a New Yorker and he certainly knew about it. His gayer friends rarely talked about anything else these days, and there was precious little gaiety involved.

Jackie didn't know exactly what had put John-Paul into the hospital. He did know that, as a gay man, his friend was a likely—a probable—subject for the gay plague. (Jackie was deeply grateful that "gay" had entered the sexual language; it was nice having a respectable word describing his friends.)

John-Paul had a totally cool mastery of himself—never apologetic or embarrassed; never eyeing any of his barracks mates—which is how he managed to get through the two years without troubles. His social circle consisted of Jackie and the other Manhattanites, and he sincerely detested the predator in the unit who was a Chaplain's Assistant.

"That chicken queen specializes in innocent country boys who've never been away from home before," he said. "They're scared to death because they're being shipped overseas. He takes them up to the choir loft and has his way with them. Predatory pederasts like him give faggotry a bad name."

Jackie didn't realize that his own body had become as tense as a closed fist until he forced it to relax at the sight of John-Paul in the room. He looked awful. He still had the prominent cheekbones that had been his chief vanity ("Roman gladiators—the ones who *defeated* their lions—all had cheekbones just like mine"). *But they were too prominent now. There seemed to be a thin film of something over his eyes, probably from the row of medications that stood by the bed in paper cups, or dripped from those ubiquitous bottles—all three of them. All of him looked dangerously fragile, a look he had never, ever, allowed himself in the years Jackie had known him. But his first words were: "It's not polite to stare. Yes, I've lost a lot of weight, for which I am grateful, but no, this isn't the method I would have chosen. And where the hell have you been?"*

Same old John-Paul.

Where Jackie had been was in Europe with a mini-series called **The Hounds of Hell***. When he started to ask John-Paul about his condition, the patient cut him off and demanded to hear all the dirt about every star Jackie had been working with.*

"Could Ronald Chesterton possibly be as gay as he looks?"

Jackie dished the dirt, as requested. Then they talked about mutual friends, and John-Paul dished. Then he disparaged hospital food with a cheerful loathing. Jackie finally demanded to know how he was doing.

"I'm dying, Jackie; how the hell do you think I'm doing?"

Jackie said the things people always say. "No, you're not dying yet, man. You're too evil to die. If you ever did there wouldn't be any virgin Seraphim left in Heaven. So stop it."

John-Paul reached out and took his friend's hand.

"Shut up, Jackie," he said. "I get to do all the talking now because I'm going to tell you something that'll shock you. Shock, but not horrify, I hope."

Jackie leaned in closer. John-Paul's energy was lower than he wanted to admit and his voice had become very soft.

"I've been in love with you for years," he said. "Did you know that?"

"Not exactly," Jackie said. "But it's not a shock. That kind of extravagant compliment was always your specialty."

Not long after John-Paul moved into the barracks, he and Jackie had spent a Sunday afternoon sitting on their footlockers and trading Broadway memories of Uta Hagen in "Who's Afraid of Virginia Woolf," Elaine Stritch in "Bus Stop," and everything Judy Garland ever did anywhere.

During a moment of silence John-Paul had said "Are you by any chance ... bi-sexual?"

Jackie said, "Uh... it's nice of you to ask, but... no."

With total aplomb, John-Paul said "Fine. Now I don't have to wonder if I should make a move. New subject."

He never alluded to it again.

"I haven't pursued the feeling because I knew I wasn't going to change you," John-Paul said. "I'm not sure I ever really wanted to."

"I've always loved you too," Jackie said, "but I think you always knew that."

"Oh, stop it! You're hopelessly hetero. You love me like you love your favorite Auntie, and that's fine. We all are who we are."

They talked on for a while, mostly remembering funny things that happened in Fort Dix days. When the meds kicked in John-Paul nodded off in the middle of a sentence. Jackie stood up, leaned over the bed, and kissed him gently on the forehead. "You're a good man, Jean-Paul," he whispered. "I'm glad I know you."

Before he got to the door, he heard the soft, rasping voice behind him. "Jackie ...wait a minute." He turned back, and found John-Paul smiling, with a distant look in his clouded eyes.

"Tell Cassie I love her, too," he said. "And tell her she'd better be nice to you or I will come back and haunt her forever."

Jackie and Cassandra Sullivan hadn't been a couple for years, but the threat was vintage John-Paul, and Jackie appreciated the thought.

Sherman Oaks, 1965

Wisdom of Ages

Jackie Barron and Cherokee McAnistan—CK to her friends—weren't in love or anything serious like that, but they met when she was a guest on the talk show that brought him back to LA in 1965, and they'd been casually intimate for almost a year.

Cherokee—who was an even six-foot tall, making her three inches taller than Jackie—was a good ol' Oklahoma gal with the rolling hills reproduced in her cheekbones. In the 50s she'd been a pin-up girl. Her popularity put her right up there with Betty Page and Diane Webber, but the 50s were over. Now she was an occasionally-working actress who had a son living with her mother back in Oklahoma, an estranged husband in New York, and a little house of her own in the San Fernando Valley.

The house came with a pool, and that's where she and Jackie generally spent their Saturday afternoons. Jackie didn't get closer than six feet away from the water since he didn't swim and had no intention of learning how. He also had no intention of working on his tan, because he didn't have one. Jackie maintained that he could get a burn sitting under a hundred-watt light bulb. He wasn't exaggerating by so very much, so he sat always under the umbrella in his lightest-weight khakis from L.L. Bean and a tee-shirt from, usually, The Raincheck Room or Kanter's Delicatessen.

Some days—like this one—they were joined by Cherokee's best friend, Jeannie, who was between boyfriends at the moment. Jackie looked absurdly overdressed next to their barely-legal bikinis, but he didn't seem to mind.

On some days—like this one—they philosophized.

"This whole *relationship* thing is all turned around," Cherokee was saying. "Women think it's disgusting when they see an older guy with some young girl. Well ... they're wrong. You take a girl of eighteen, say. If she's still a virgin—and *I* was, dammit—she doesn't know the first thing about sex, and some heavy-breathing boy is not the somebody who's going to treat her right. A girl shouldn't ought to learn about making love in the back seat of a car."

"I don't know, CK," Jeannie said. "Eighteen year old boys may be a little clumsy, but by God they're *adorable*, you've got admit that."

Jeannie was an attractive dancer and Cherokee's best friend. She kept her streaming hair a jet black—a nice contrast to Cherokee's platinum blonde—because she was working with a Polynesian-dance company at a West Hollywood restaurant called The Tiki-Taki. It was Jackie's guess that she was probably an unacknowledged few years older than Cherokee.

Cherokee herself was so scornful of the Hollywood habit of dodging the question of age that she would announce herself as thirty-nine at any opportunity.

"Ah, but that's different," CK said. "Now you're talking about *you*, and it's been a few weeks at least since *you* were eighteen. I'm talking about a young girl who doesn't know missionary position from reverse-cowgirl. A boy her own age is probably going to be so damn clumsy it could take her years to get into the swing of it. No, it ought to be normal practice for a girl who's just starting out to connect up with a man who's at least pushing forty. A *gentleman* pushing forty, of course, not some wham-bam-thank-you-ma'am pervert. *He'll* know what the hell he's doing, he'll take her to dinner some place nice and talk sweet and slow to her, and by God he'll send her flowers the next morning. And he won't be writing her phone number on the Boys Room wall."

"Damn, CK," Jeannie said, "what kind of boys did you *know* in high school?"

Jackie, who was the only one present who had actually been a boy in high school, sat quietly. He was ten years short of forty, so he had nothing to gain from Cherokee's logic.

"Honey, it was the boys I knew in high school who taught me to stay away from boys in high school," she said. "You take that gentleman in his forties, he's probably a little more comfortable with himself, so he's got time to concentrate on treating a girl right. Besides which, he's probably learned a lot from other women, and he can use that tender knowledge with the newcomer. It's ideal."

It was time for Jackie to contribute to the conversation. "Excuse me," he said, "but have we forgotten that I'm here? Do I not exist in this time-twisting sexual universe?"

"Don't worry," CK said, "I'm getting to you. The opposite's true for a woman. A *woman* who's sneaking up on forty—like me, for instance—is *ready* for a younger man. You can have a damn fine time training an eighteen-year-old so's he can be ready for whomsoever he's going to marry eventually." She stopped, leaned over, and patted Jackie gently on his unexposed thigh.

"Did I get that *whomsoever* right?" she said.

Jackie shrugged. "Truth is—I'm damned if I know. But I love the way you say it."

She turned triumphantly to Jeannie. "You see what I mean? How you gonna not love a man who talks like that? Fortunately for me, this age thing isn't only just for teenagers. I've never met a man who couldn't learn a few things if he'd just pay attention to the older but wiser woman. Like me. And Jackie does, bless his sweet little heart."

"I'm always eager to learn," Jackie said. "I figure studying with an international sex symbol is just about as good as it gets."

"Damn rights," Cherokee said. "What do I need with a man my own age? I'll be forty next year, and a woman's at her sexual peak at this age. Which is about at the level of a seventeen year old boy. *That* combination would make good sense—except that the only seventeen-year-old I know is my son, and I am not considering that as a sexual statement."

Jeannie raised her hand. "*I'm* not related to him," she said. "When's he coming out here to visit you again?"

"Never you damn mind," Cherokee said. "You're my best friend, so that would make it incest by proxy. Or something like that. You find your own seventeen-year-old."

"Uh ... CK?" Jackie said. "I'm not seventeen. Am I leaning on doddering-old-man hood to you?"

"Absolutely not," she said. "Far as that goes, I don't even know how old you are. You've got a good job and you've already been in the Army, so I'm thinking at least twenty-five. Twenty-six?"

"I've always tried to combine an old soul with a young face," Jackie said. "I'm thirty. Can I squeeze by on that??"

"All right; that's a little older than I thought, but you've still got the energy of a kid in bed, so you've got some time left. But I think thirty-one's a reasonable cut-off point; don't you? After that you can concentrate on those young girls; they need a man who's been trained by a woman who already knows what he should be doing."

"Can I have him when he hits thirty-two, CK?" Jeannie said.

Cherokee let a silence take over for a moment before saying, "Well ... speaking of who's got him and who's gonna have him ... I'm gonna take that as my cue to get into the unpleasant part of the afternoon."

She stopped and looked directly at Jackie. "You know my husband's been doing that musical on Broadway. Well, he called last night, darlin'," she said. "The show closed and he's moving out here to take a shot at being a movie star. And he thinks we ought to get back together. He may be right; I don't know. We've talked about it before. I guess we ought to give it a try."

Jeannie was struck dumb and it took Jackie a long moment to respond. "Uh ... you do have an .... *unusual* way of breaking news," he said.

Cherokee shrugged. "You and me been a good couple, but we were never really going to be a *couple*, you know? I don't see you as married, and I damn sure don't see you as my son's stepfather. Besides, like I said, it's about time for you to spread the wisdom to the next generation. You're not going to make this end *bad*, are you?"

It took less than a moment's thought for Jackie to realize that there was no way he was going to make this end badly. They'd had some terrific months, and now it was her husband's turn. *He* was well past thirty-one, but no one ever accused Cherokee of being consistent.

There wasn't much more to the conversation after that. Jackie finished his beer, made a date to see her for dinner on Monday for a proper farewell, and kissed her seriously but innocently, the way a caring now-former lover should.

As he walked away from the pool he bent over to give Jeannie a proper goodbye peck on the cheek.

Jeannie said, "So long, kiddo," turning slightly away from CK. Extending her thumb and little finger in a universal sign for *telephone*, she angled her face up so she could look Jackie in the eye and silently mouthed *call me*.

By the time he got to the freeway, Jackie was wondering if Cherokee and her husband were really getting back together or if she was just looking for a way to end things without hurting his feelings. She did have good manners.

He was also wondering what the respectful waiting period was before calling your ex-girlfriend's best friend.

He was pretty sure that in L.A. time it wasn't very long.

New York, 1975

Everything In Its Place

Getting through his door was the easy part. Jackie Barron had been getting through the door in this condition for enough years that it almost never took more than three tries to get the key into the lock.

His task once he got inside would probably be a little trickier. But not much. There were only a few places the picture could be. Unless he'd lost it over the years. And that couldn't be. The picture would be there. Somewhere. Had to be.

Jackie was weaving a little where he stood; first just inside the door, then leaning back against it. Which stopped the weaving. Good move.

Okay, he mumbled. *Only one place it could be. Got to be in the file cabinet. I'll just dig it out. No big deal.*

He used both arms to push away from the door, which caused a loss of balance (which hadn't been too firm to begin with) which sent him stumbling to his left, into the coffee-table. Jerking away from this collision sent him to his right and almost into the television set. Bad move, but at least the top of the TV provided a surface high enough for steadying himself. Almost nothing is all bad.

Jackie glanced around his living room while he waited for body and mind to get back into sync. The room hadn't changed any since he left that morning. Cassie Sullivan had complained that it was like living in a library. A dysfunctional library where nobody had gotten around to shelving the stacked books for a year or so. Where there was no more shelf-space for books. Where there was no more wall-space for shelves. Funny it bothered her that way. Didn't bother Jackie. The books were still there but she wasn't.

With balance semi-fully reclaimed, Jackie stepped carefully across the room, his hands extended like a tightrope-walker. *I can do this. No big deal.*

He arrived at the desk that wasn't really a desk. The top had been born to be a door, but it hadn't worked out that way. In 1966, when he bought it, would-be doors often wound up topping two file cabinets to create the creative man's desk. The householder's equivalent of the college boy's bookcase made of boards laid across stacked bricks.

I bet I'm the last guy in New York with a desk like this, Jackie thought. *Maybe in America*. He shrugged to himself. *Or else not. Do I care?*

Jackie pulled open the bottom drawer on the right-hand cabinet, which was a particularly unappealing shade of brown. The drawer stuck and then sagged as he pulled it out. *Damn thing's getting old*, Jackie thought. *Probably born old. Like me. Hee hee.*

The folder he sought was in the back; all the way in the back, behind Insurance and Bank and Letters and Medical. It was plain manila, and it held far more photographs and documents than it was meant to hold. It held his past. This folder was what he would run into a burning building to save.

All right, Miss Fionnuala, he thought, *You're not lost. Nothing's lost. I know you're in here. You and your five little playmates. Got to be here. You know the rules.*

Jackie was aware, not for the first time, of the unfair power of the past. He'd gone drinking this evening with

Mark Berger, a friend he hadn't seen in twenty years. He was glad to see Mark, they'd been drinking companions in college days and that shared interest hadn't changed. They caught up quickly with the mandatory what-have-you-been-up-tos, and then, like any young men with a shared educational background, they spent the rest of the evening revisiting memories of a more intensely meaningful matter: the girls they had known. Jackie's end of the conversation centered on *girl*, singular. Mark had been his closest friend when he was more deeply in love than he'd ever been, and that was the girl Jackie felt like remembering.

Jackie had met her in 1954, in college, and been intrigued by her name: Fionnuala ... *Petkoglu*? *Bzzzzzt! Wrong!*

But that was her name. Her father's name was Ioannis Petkoglu. The thoughtful bureaucrats at Ellis Island had changed it to Johnny Peters for him when he immigrated from Salonica in the twenties and he changed it right back as soon as he was old enough to go to court. As Professor Petkoglu he was now an intimidating man who taught physics at UCLA. Her mother was a Boston Irish immigrant named Kathleen Hawkins, who was fair-to-medium beautiful and dangerously playful. Kathleen Hawkins Petkoglu thought it would be pretty funny to have a daughter named Fionnuala Petkoglu. By the time the child was old enough to go to school, the name had ceased to be amusing. Except to the other children, who thought it was hilarious. Even teachers generally had to be stopped from calling her some variation of *Fi-oh-nu-allah*; they were eventually able to memorize *Fee-NOO-la*, but her classmates preferred calling her *Fionnielala.* Even as a child she did not suffer fools gladly, and hearing *Fionnielala* from others often resulted in a punch from *Fee-NOO-la.* Fortunately, Jackie was nineteen by the time they met, and he was so smitten that he not only pronounced Fionnuala properly, he learned to spell it right. And he loved the *Petkoglu* part; the syllables bounced on his tongue like a ping-pong ball in play.

But this evening's problem did not concern her name. It concerned her picture. He sat down carefully on his rolling desk-chair. He removed everything from the folder—this wasn't hard; the folder was falling apart—and started searching from the very top. The first thing there was a strip of photos of an actress he once knew; pictures shot from a television screen when she made an appearance on a daytime show.

This shouldn't be here, he mumbled. *This shouldn't be on top. She was a long time ago. How long ago? Lemme see. It had to be —whoa. Why do I care? We're looking for Fionnuala here. Keep going.*

Before he left Los Angeles, Jackie had been besotted with Fionnuala, who was a child prodigy and already in college at the age of fifteen. She was not besotted with him—an omission he bitterly regretted then and forever after—but he was someone she could talk to without holding anything back. He accepted and hated this. She could tell him about the lover she had outgrown; the lover who had left her pregnant before she left him flat.

Jackie had moved to New York before the baby was born, but they wrote to each other all the time. And she sent him the picture that he had to find tonight. Had to.

It was not as easy as he had expected. He went to the bottom of the stack, where the photo chronologically should be but wasn't.

He glanced quickly at the pictures, one at a time, before resting them against his chest. Sometimes he slowed down. *Here's the cast of that play I did in college. Only I'm not in the picture. That must mean something.*

The pictures were of varying sizes—some weren't even pictures. There were crumbling clips from newspapers or magazines concerning something or someone he'd been involved with somehow or other, and when he was almost halfway down the stack the whole pile slid off his lap and scattered across the floor. When he bent to gather them up the desk chair rolled backwards from under him and he went to his knees the hard way. He didn't bother getting back up.

Who am I kidding. It's not here. Hasn't been here for years.

When his thoughts became audible, Jackie was no longer just mumbling. He was seriously talking to himself now. *I'm lookin' and I'm findin'. Here's Oliver mopping the latrine in the Army. Here's those cheesecake shots of Joni I taped up in my locker at Fort Dix; I pretended she was my girlfriend. Nobody believed it.*

He was flipping through his past much more rapidly now, desperation almost clearing up his thinking. *Here's the picture of me that girl from Boston drew. God, she was weird. Here's—here's not what I need. Here's not Fionnuala . Godammit, it's gone! She's gone. How could I do that? How could I lose—*

And there she was. Fionnuala Petkoglu, grinning the amazing grin that hypnotized him when he was nineteen years old. She was holding an ice-cream cone; standing with five other girls from Evangeline House, the home where she and all the other unwed mothers-to-be had gone to have their babies and put them up for immediate adoption away from neighborhood scrutiny. That's the way the best families did it in the 50s.

Six teenage girls together; giggling and holding their ice-cream cones up like Olympic trophies. Schoolgirls on an afternoon lark at the ice-cream parlor. All of them adorable. All of them with puffy faces and hugely pregnant bellies. Fionnuala had loved the startled reactions they got from passersby when they were allowed to go out of Sanger House together on Wednesday afternoons.

Life is good, Jackie said aloud as he studied the picture of a young and, at that moment, happy mother-to-be who would never see her baby.

This picture isn't lost, he thought. *It's in my hand.*

Fionnuala isn't lost, he thought. *She's in my head. Where she belongs.*

Jackie Barron put the picture where *it* belonged—at the very foundation of the stack, where his earliest treasures ought to be. Still dressed, he laid himself on his bed, where he slept soundly and dreamed sweetly. But not, oddly enough, of Fionnuala Petkoglu.

New York, 1981

More in Anger

Before he left to work in London for ten weeks, Jackie Barron told Virginia-called-Jinx Michaels that he would write to her every day. It was one of those corny things that young lovers used to say in the black and white movies he grew up on.

In 1981 there weren't any more black and white movies and, at 46, Jackie wasn't all that young anymore. But he wrote to her every day anyway, usually in sweetly salacious images.

During the last weeks away he had trouble concentrating on the job. He counted the days until he would be back in New York. The day before he left London he trimmed his fingernails very carefully, so that he wouldn't accidentally injure any of her more tender parts.

Jinx wasn't at the airport to meet him because he arrived at 3 a.m., but she was waiting by the door at her new apartment on Bleecker Street that afternoon. God was in his heaven, all was right with the world.

And then everything turned to shit.

She tried to ease into it. She showed him her new home, four rooms below street level in the Village; big living room (by Village standards), small bedroom (by any standards), none of the furniture they had rolled around on in her old place.

Her eyes were welcoming but wary. She kissed him, but it was dutiful.

Bad signs. Now what?

Jinx sat him down in the armchair and settled herself on the edge of the couch.

"There isn't any good way to say this," she said badly. "I told you about Ted Tanner when we were first together. I told you how I felt about him. It wasn't a secret."

The name was a sore point with Jackie. "Yes, Jinx, you told me about him. Often. I'm back ten minutes and *he's* what you want to talk about?"

The edge to Jackie's voice was not natural to him with anyone; certainly not with Jinx. She'd been the first—almost the first—woman in his life after his divorce last year, and he was pretty sure he loved her. Ted Tanner had fucked her and forsaken her before Jackie ever knew her.

"Please don't be mad," she said. "It's not my fault. I never lied to you; I didn't say this was forever or anything like that. Did I?" Jackie heard a lot of pity and a little condescension in her tone. He didn't like it.

"Godammit, Jinx, don't tell me what you didn't do; tell me what you *did* do! Why are we talking about that weasel?"

"He's not a weasel. The irony is, you'd probably like him if you knew him. He's an actor and he's restless ... but he's showed up again. And he loves me."

"Loves you! Jesus Christ, Jinx; he's a self-styled ladies-man who took off for L.A. and he bangs anything that can't outrun him. You think I didn't ask around about him? My friend Rafe was the number one swordsman on Sunset Boulevard until Ted fucking Tanner showed up. He told me all about this guy who *loves* you. He's a prick, Jinx, and if he's calling you again—whatever he tells you about anything—he's lying. Just hang up on him."

"He's not a prick and he's not just calling or writing—he's here. We were in that bedroom for 24 hours straight and he stayed until I made him leave because you were coming. He's in New York for a week and he loves me! He hasn't said so yet, but he will. I *hate* hurting you, Jackie; you're a nice man, but Teddy and I belong together and now he knows it, too. I *know* he knows it!"

Jinx was still being very slick-paper-magazine; very Lauren Bacall. She had made coffee for them but both cups were on the table untouched. Jackie had stopped smoking while he was in Europe, but he picked up her Marlboro pack, ripped it open, took out a cigarette and lit it.

He let the silence sit on the room before speaking again. Jinx was breathing hard and he could see her breasts moving up and down under the thin sweater. He remembered the silicone "improvement "her body had rejected. She had never liked her breasts very much but he did.

"I don't get it," he said. "I don't get it. We've got something going here, and you can't just kiss me off like this. You said the one rule you had was that if I was with you there couldn't be anybody else; not in any way. I kept my part of the deal, godammit!"

This wasn't exactly true, but pretty close.

"Do you think I like this?" she said, crushing out her own cigarette. "I'm not saying you did anything wrong. You're a good guy, and I'm not saying Ted is a better one. But he's the *right* one, Jackie—can't you just accept that?"

"No, I can't just accept that. He's done this to you before; he'll do it again. What's the *matter* with you!"

"Nothing! What I'm doing to you isn't nice, and I know it, but I'm not sure being *nice* is what life's all about!"

Her smile became smug beyond endurance when she said, "This time next year I'll be Mrs. Ted Tanner, Jackie. I just know it."

Jackie let the silence descend again, and held it until her smile became a little less Mona Lisa. When he finally spoke, he spoke softly, calmly.

"He *said* that, did he? He said 'I can't live without you, Virginia; I need you to be Mrs. Me'? Or did he just say 'come here and *do* me one more time,' and *you* decided marriage was the hidden message? Jesus, Jinx; you're too *bright* for that!"

Now she let the silence settle in until *she* could speak with some control.

"I've done a bad thing to you, Jackie. I never meant to. You're entitled to be mad. I'm a selfish *cunt*. But you know what? That's how it's got to be. I feel really, really bad for you, because you deserve better. But it's my *life* we're talking about."

Jackie took another cigarette, tucked it in his pocket, stood up, and put on his jacket.

"My life, too, *Virginia*. And don't call yourself a cunt; your cunt is *pretty* and what you're *doing* is ugly. Worse yet, it's stupid."

He reached into his shoulder bag and took out a necklace he had brought for her.

"Keep this, sell it, give it away, stick it up your ass in remembrance of me. I don't care." The necklace only cost $12 in the Portobello market, but she didn't know that.

"You're making a big, big mistake," he said. "I made a bigger one when I got involved. Have a good life, but don't count on having it with Tanner."

Jackie stopped for a moment to examine his own feelings after he climbed the stone steps that led to the sidewalk.

Okay, he said to himself. *Okay. This time I'm the injured party. I'm the innocent victim. I'm not the villain of the piece. I've got nothing to feel guilty about. For once.*

God damn. That part feels good.

New York, 2008

Taps

The Greek Orthodox priest wore a long black robe and a long black beard and he kept chanting and singing *Oh Lord, have mercy on us, Oh Lord, have mercy on us.* Finally he said...*and forgive ... uh ... this beloved person...* because, for a moment, he couldn't think of Nick Christoforos's name. Nick hadn't been in a church since his mother's funeral.

This would have amused the hell out of Nick, since people were always screwing up his name. In his absence, Jackie Barron was amused for him. It would be a great story to tell the old friends who couldn't be there.

Nick wasn't totally absent. His remains were in the pewter vase that stood in front of the cross in the funeral parlor room. His passion in life had been Broadway and the movies; after the Memorial his son would keep a promise he'd made his father. He was going to scatter Nick's ashes just slightly off Broadway, in Shubert Alley.

Nick was born in Bridgeport, but his immigrant parents weren't, and they had named him Ioannes Nikolaos Christoforos. Since no one could pronounce that name in Bridgeport, he became Nick. Jackie had met him when they were both in the peacetime Army, stationed at Fort Dix and—like Nick's relatives—he usually called him Nikos. (*Private First Class Nikos* when they were being more formal.)

When the eulogies began Jackie was going to speak about those playing-soldier years—Nick's description—and he had gathered together as many of the 1958-60 Army crowd as he could. It had been forty-eight years since they got out, but people didn't forget Nick Christoforos.

The ungrizzled veterans included Franz Laurentia, a poet-playwright who'd always been assigned to menial labor during the peacetime-warrior years.

"I wrote a play making fun of the Army when Nick had a theater in a Service Club," Laurentia told Janice, Nick's niece. "Nick was the star—he was always the star. He played a lunatic modeled on the Regiment Commander, and there was a good chance we'd all wind up in front of a Court Martial. As it turned out, everything was cool because the Colonel who was in charge of everything heard what we were doing. He snuck in to a performance one night and laughed his ass off. After that he had Nick transferred to work in his office. Being a Colonel can get pretty boring."

Sal Minucci, built like the sanitation truck he drove in Newark these days, had worked in the First Division Motor Pool. When he answered the phone in the motor pool office he always said "Number Truckin' One—Pvt. Minucci speaking," and got away with it.

Gerry van der Heuvel never made it into the Drum & Bugle Corps at Fort Dix, but now he was a successful jazz trumpet player. He wasn't much of a talker, but Nick—who didn't know the first thing about jazz—could always get him started by asking questions about Miles Davis, or Dizzy Gillespie. Gerry was sitting by himself in the back, with a trumpet case under his seat.

Sal was sitting with Gary Foster Billingham, a Washington lobbyist who had been the defense counsel when Nick was once charged with showing *disrespect to a commissioned officer*. A young Lieutenant had taken offense when Nick's hand made a jerky pattern in the air like a maddened mime when he raised it to salute. The Colonel himself testified on Nick's behalf, insisting that he was just rehearsing a play and meant no disrespect. Nobody actually believed that, but nobody challenges a Colonel.

"Did you see van der Heuvel back there?" Sal whispered. "Seven to five he's gonna play *Taps*." Sal would bet on how many Styrofoam cups were on the floor of an OTB office.

When everybody was seated, Irini—Nick's oldest friend—was first up.

"We used to visit relatives in Hell's Kitchen every summer," she said. "My people were Romanian, and I taught Nick a little of the language. He loved the curses; he said they sounded like an angry man clearing vomit out of his throat. His favorite was *Your mother should have thrown you out with the afterbirth!* And it sounds even worse in Romanian."

Bernice, a schoolteacher he met after his divorce, was up next. She spoke of the 8mm movie Nick shot with all his friends over a two year period.

"I wound up as a nun turned stripper with my skirt up over my head. Nick was a total madman, which is why we all loved him," she said. "Does everybody remember the scavenger hunts he used to organize? One night Irini and I had to bring back a fish head, page 25 from a Danbury telephone book, and a used condom. That last one wasn't as easy as you'd think."

Jackie was determined to keep his oration brief, so he talked about the problem sergeants had with Nick's last name. That was something he knew every Kazantakas and Antonescu in the room would identify with.

"For some reason they couldn't get their tongues around ChrisTOWforos," he said. "They called him just plain Christopher, or CHRIST-o-fouros, or CristoFOROS. That's until he went to work for the Colonel. They learned to pronounce his name real fast after that."

Janice, who had been more than a niece to Nick ever since she was a child, closer to him than anyone outside his own son and grandchildren, was the last formal speaker. She almost got through without crying.

"My uncle Nick told about a thousand people about taking me to see *My Fair Lady* when I was seven," she recalled happily. "At the intermission he asked me if I knew what the show was about and I said 'At first they didn't like the lady because her face was all dirty, but when they cleaned her up they found out she could sing and dance, and then they liked her a lot.' Uncle Nick loved that story; said it was the only realistic description of a musical he'd ever heard.

"He was always introducing me to something new. He knew the doorman at a cabaret called the *Bon Soir*, and when I was eleven he slipped me in to hear Barbra Streisand. She was only seven years older than me."

When the formalities were over no one wanted to leave, and the friends kept talking. They remembered that Nick, who interviewed celebrities for a living, often confounded actors by remembering their careers better than they did. He had a shelf full of books lovingly inscribed to him by people ranging from Lucille Ball to Gore Vidal.

They remembered him starring as the villain in a children's musical when he was an actor pretending to sing. Judging the Miss USA contest. Escorting his friend Debbie to Bellevue each time she made another half-hearted attempt at suicide.

When the Nick stories were—not finished; never finished; just halted—Gerry van der Heuvel started walking up from the back with his muted trumpet in his hand.

"Did I tell you?" Sal Minucci said. "It's gonna be *Taps* for the old soldier; just like that guy in *FromHere to Eternity.*"

Van der Heuvel was playing softly as he walked. Almost everybody in the room recognized the melody, and it wasn't *Taps*.

It was Noel Coward.

If there was someone playing the piano at a party—Nick never missed a party—Nick would sing Coward's song, with a wistful, nameless longing for something that had never quite happened for him.

No one ever teased him about it.

The song ends: *I believe that since my life began/The most I've had is just a talent to amuse...*

That wasn't literally true, but everyone understood why it brought out the intensity in Nick, and why it was proper. His talent to amuse never flagged, even this year, when everyone knew that death was the approaching punchline.

After the muted trumpet faded away they began gathering up their coats. Nick's people inhabited a wide variety of worlds, and they knew they would never again be all together in one room like this.

The stories were through—but they would get told again and yet again, at least until everyone in the room was dead.

New York, 1968

Searching for the Key, It Is Always Three O'Clock in the Morning

"Was I in here tonight?"

For a brief and disgusted moment the bartender looked at Jackie Barron, who was weaving as he leaned over the top of the bar. The bartender remembered the unsteady would-be customer. He remembered refusing to serve him.

"Yeah, pal. You were in here. For a New York minute. I told you to get lost then and I'm telling you now. Go on back to where you got loaded in the first place."

"No no," Jackie Barron said. "I don't want a drink. Really. Just need to find my keys. And I'm sorry if I made a disturbance."

"You weren't here long enough to make a disturbance. The door's back there where it was when you came in. Goodbye."

"Gimme break, okay? I lost my keys. Little skinny key-ring; two keys on it? Jus' lemme look around; see if I lost it here. Can I look around?"

"No need to, pal, you weren't here long enough to get anything or lose anything, either. It's 3 a.m. and that's going-home time. Don't make me *toss* you out."

"God Almighty, man, I just want to look around! I just need the key to my apartment. I don't care about the other one. You could keep that one."

The bartender came around the bar, took Jackie by the arm—not gently—and walked him towards the door. "I don't care what you don't care about," the bartender said.

"I got no more patience with you. You're not even a regular. Do your talkin' walkin'." Jackie didn't resist.

Once outside, he steadied himself on the back of a bench that was chained to the front of the small store next door. He sat down slowly, carefully, and lit another cigarette.

"Wouldn't have been there anyway," he mumbled. "It's not anywhere. Fucking key disappeared. 'Vaporated. Ain't that just like a key?"

Jackie ran his hands into the pockets of his coat once more—fortieth time, maybe—and again came out with nothing more substantial than his cigarettes, his lighter and a slightly used Kleenex. He unzipped the bag that hung from his shoulder and took everything out—also for the fortieth time, maybe. Two manila folders, unopened Marlboros, a book and two ballpoint pens. The keys hadn't miraculously appeared.

"I can't ring the Super," he said, louder than he intended. A man walking by heard him and walked on a little faster. "Three in the morning. Can't ring his bell again. He's pissed off from the last time."

On this dark night Jackie was making his way back towards the office where he worked, checking any bar that seemed even remotely familiar. On Manhattan's West Side in the 70s the prospects seemed endless. He had gone first to the Savor Bar, where he was pretty sure he had been. He was right.

"Sure you were here," the bartender said. "You really don't remember?"

"I'm just looking for my keys," Jackie said.

"You don't remember Phyllis, down the end of the bar?" The bartender jerked his head to the right and Jackie saw a middle-aged woman who was neither attractive nor homely. Just there.

"You thought she was hot stuff a couple hours ago," the bartender said. "I was glad; I thought maybe she was finally gonna get lucky." The bartender snorted. "Then she started talking about her boss and how a woman's not got a chance in business. You left as fast as everybody else does."

"I sat with her? I'll go look there for my keys."

"No, I tell you what–you check the floor here; this is where you sat first. I'll go check around Phyllis; I think you hurt her feelings. Just stay here."

Jackie dropped to one knee and ran his hand along the floor. Nothing more solid than cigarette butts. Most of them probably his. By the time he was able to stand up more-or-less straight again, the bartender was back.

"Naw, nothing there. And Phyllis says you're a chauvinist pig."

Jackie walked to the door under his own guidance this time. He took a cab–two passed him by–to a 57th Street bar that he didn't like very much but sometimes stopped in anyway. Nobody there knew anything about any keys.

Nobody knew anything about any keys at any of the half-dozen saloons he visited. Three of the bartenders assured him that he hadn't been there anyway. His last hope was the Broadcast Grill, right around the corner from the network that employed him. He remembered going there with friends after work, staying behind when they left to go home.

At the Broadcast Grill he was welcomed. Joanie, his regular waitress, brought him a Johnnie Walker Black on the rocks, then got a flashlight and searched carefully and seriously. No keys. She offered to find him a cab.

"No cab," Jackie said. "Can't go home without my key. No point."

"Well, you can't stay here, Jackie. We're closing in about ten minutes."

"Pay-phone," he said. "One call and then I'm gone. Swear to God."

He dialed a number; after several rings a voice thick with sleep said "Hello?"

"Cassandra, it's Jackie. Do you still have your key to my apartment?"

"Are you crazy? Four o'clock in the morning you're worrying that I might still have your key? What—I'm going to *rob* you?"

"No no no; I lost my key; I can't get in. You're my last chance, baby."

"You've already had your last chance, *baby*. Ten times. I threw away the damn key when I threw away your pictures. And don't call me again!"

When she put down the phone she was not gentle. Jackie winced and thought of a solution. He could stop looking and sleep around the corner.

Getting into the network headquarters was not a problem; he flashed his ID card, scrawled his name in the Sign-In book, and the guard waved him through. The elevator took him straight to the 18th floor.

"Brilliant," he was thinking. "Clean shirt and tie for tomorrow—today—in my desk. Couch and a clock in Eli's office. Problem solved."

Eli Manning III, the Vice-President of Press Relations, never locked the door of his office. Jackie could set the alarm clock, get a few hours sleep on the couch, and be out of there long before anyone else showed up. Fabulous plan.

When he turned to walk from the boss's desk to the couch, his right foot collided with his left ankle and he tumbled to the floor. The carpet was soft, but he said "Argh!" when his right knee hit on something small and hard.

He had landed on the bottom hem of his coat. The keys were there, inside the lining.

"No no," Jackie mumbled. "Cannot be. I do not put keys in that pocket. Never. That pocket's got a hole in it. Jesus H."

Jackie didn't bother standing back up. He crawled carefully to the couch, sat down and leaned his back against it.

"This can't keep happening," he said out loud. "Got to stop. No more. No more no mores. Tomorrow morning—no, tomorrow night—tomorrow I'll go to the goddamn church basement with all the other losers. I'll go to their goddamn *meeting* and put an end to this shit. For good.

"Tomorrow."

Van Nuys, 1965

It Ain't What You Do, It's the Way What You Do It

"If you walk in and see a whole bunch of naked people, don't let it make you nervous. That's the dress-code on this job."

Corinna DeVegh enjoyed rattling Jackie a little when they made the appointment to meet in Canoga Park on the set of *Sleepy Daze Triple-X Nights*. It was her latest hard-core movie, and she had always enjoyed upsetting his balance. They had been lovers in her New York days—three years ago, when she only starred in soft-core movies with no penetration. On one memorable occasion she had dropped her napkin and followed it under the table at Jim Downey's restaurant on Eighth Avenue. She giggled while she unzipped his trousers. They'd both been drinking, so it seemed funny at the time. He asked her later if she would have gone through with it if he hadn't jumped up. She just smiled and told him he'd never know. And that it would be his turn next time.

Life had never been *ordinary* with Corinna, but walking onto this porn-movie set in 1965 was an uneasy experience for Jackie all the same. She had assured him that he was in no danger of being arrested—everything going on in the building was illegal, but the producer regularly crossed the appropriate palms, and they'd never been raided.

It had been her idea for Jackie to interview her for the LA Free Press. The TV network that employed him as a publicist wouldn't approve, but he kept his sanity by doing a little free-lance journalism on the side.

He spotted her as soon as he walked in after being cleared by a dangerously over-built black man who seemed larger than the door he was guarding. There were, as promised, naked bodies in evidence, but Corinna was wearing a midnight-blue cocktail dress and relaxing. Her scene would be coming up next.

She hadn't changed much, still defying the obsession with blondes that dominated movies both clean and dirty. Her hair was the same wildfire it had always been, only now she had it cropped tight around her face, like Shirley MacLaine's. Even fully dressed, her breasts made the other girls on the set look like lady gymnasts. There had never been any question of implants—Corinna unaided was the *After* look that the silicone-sellers dreamed of.

She had already been a pro—within limits—when she left New York to sample the waters of Hollywood. She hadn't drowned in those waters, but she'd gotten her feet a little wetter than she had expected to. In New York she'd become established as *Catherine the Great, Gorgon of the Gulag*. After *Catherine II, III, IV and V*, she was very well-known in the soft-core industry, specializing in despicable acts of torture and outrageous sex-orgies with guards and prisoners. They were all simulated.

In her Hollywood movies (actually filmed in the San Fernando Valley) there was no sadism —she was never going to be the Gorgon again—and the sex wasn't simulated. She had become a XXX superstar called Sativa Sharone.

A mutual friend had given him her number, and she was delighted when he called. Their breakup really had nothing to do with her devotion to her work, Jackie accepted that. The breakup had to do with Jackie's devotion to his next drink and his ever-increasing inability to handle the previous one. There was no such thing as a woman Corinna couldn't compete with, but even she was no match for Jack Daniel's. Their parting wasn't pretty, but they genuinely liked each other, so they got over it.

Corinna hugged him hard—the Corinna he knew; not the Sativa he'd read about—and took him back to a tiny office that was as close to a dressing room as she had. Jackie knew an assistant director could take her away at any time, so he whipped out a notebook and got to business.

But the former Corinna took charge of the interview in an unexpectedly chipper manner. "You think there's a big difference between hard-core and the fake stuff in *Gorgon*, right? You want to know why I decided to fuck for a living," she said.

"Well ... yeah."

"That's a fair question," she said. "But stupid. Thank you for asking. Have I gotten fat since you saw me last? Or skinny? Have my tits dropped or my arms started to sag or my teeth turned yellow?"

"Uh ... definitely not. So ...?"

"You know why not? Because I was given some nice presents at birth and I work hard to keep them that way. Just like you. You were born with a little talent, and you write, and you work and think hard to keep your mind in shape, right?"

"Well... more or less... ."

"Whore," she said. "You're using what nature gave you to make money. You don't have much respect for what you do, but you also do every damn thing you can to be known as the best one doing it. Right?"

"Right again," he said. "Am I going to do any questioning here?"

"No. You don't have to. Today we'll use *my* mind. Maybe afterwards we'll put your body to work. How does that sound?"

"Sounds great." He didn't try to say anything more.

"If we do—do you think it'll be the same as what I do for the camera this afternoon? When you used to write me love letters—were they the same as the press-releases you write, praising some crap you wouldn't dream of watching if you weren't getting paid to? Or is there a difference between who you are and what you do?"

"Point," he said.

"Of course, point. I'm a very smart girl, Jackie. You contributed to that. I didn't have to go to college—being around you made me want to find out who on earth Kurt Vonnegut and Philip Roth and Jack Kerouac were. I read Alan Watts and *Zen in the Art of Archery* and all that stuff, same as you did. I learned from you. And I bet your body learned from me. Right?"

Jackie just said, "Oh, yes." His voice was cloudy.

"Damn right. We do what we do best, Jackie. All of us. But I don't get sexually transmitted diseases, and you don't talk or think like a pompous ass who worships stupid TV shows. We avoid the traps and we stay independent. Right?"

"Yes, *Corinna*; we do, and I see your point, but—"

"No *butts*. I don't do anal. I don't apologize for one minute for what I do, but I just don't choose to do that. It's probably just because I'm afraid it'll hurt; it's not because I think it's wrong. I wouldn't do it with you for love so I certainly don't do it with them for a *movie*. I decide what the boundaries are.

"Now," she said. "Tell me again what brings you out here. What are you working on?"

"Same old shit," he said. "Publicist for a show that is so god-awful I figure it'll be cancelled and I'll go back to New York before the summer is over. I left my overcoat stored in the basement of McGovern's Tavern. Paddy sends his love."

"So you're working on a show you hate," she said. "And you're going to write lies, saying it's terrific." She shrugged and spread her hands. "Using your mind to do what somebody pays you to do. In public. But you make a more-or-less honest living, and you don't really hate the job *all* the time, do you? Sometimes it's fun, isn't it?"

"How on earth did I last with you as long as I did?" he said. "You're merciless!"

"That's right," she said, "I am. Now, you sit here and write a colorful description of what I'm about to do out there. Just make it up—you're not going to watch me shoot the scene. I told you I have boundaries."

At the door, she turned back as both Corinna and Sativa.

"Tonight, you leave your degeneracy at the network and I'll leave mine here," she said. "When we get to my house ... I can read you the haiku I've been writing, and you can fuck a porn star.

"Life don't get no better than that, Jackie Barron."

New York, 1976

First Time; First Step

There was a fine irony involved when Jackie Barron walked into the familiar church basement on a Monday night. Sometimes that basement was a community theater—a term that always seemed incongruous when applied to a theater in Manhattan. For twenty years that theater was where he could play at being a director, a man of importance, rehearsing plays by night and forgetting his day job.

But never on a Monday night. On Monday nights the basement was not a theater; on Monday nights it was a meeting room for Alcoholics Anonymous.

Jackie had always resented the fact that, no matter how near a show might be to opening night, no matter how desperately the cast might need that extra night's rehearsal on stage, there could be no exception. Monday nights belonged to AA; subject closed.

Now he was standing in the basement on a Monday night for the first time; unsteady but standing. And the irony wasn't amusing.

He hadn't expected to see anyone he knew there, but the first person he saw when he walked in was Drew Lawrence. They'd been drinking companions when they worked together; then drinking became more important than working to Drew, and after a while he wasn't working with anyone. Jackie had seen him off and on over the years since. Drew had stopped drinking and started a new life, and this was puzzling because he didn't match the popular image of self-pitying losers in Alcoholics Anonymous. He was the same Drew he'd always been, but without the slurring.

"Jackie! Is it tacky for me to say I'm glad to see you here? How long?"

Jackie looked quickly around the room to see if there were any other familiar faces that he did not want to see. There weren't.

"No, no—it's not what you think, Drew. I'm just here to look around. That's all."

"Sit over here with me," Drew said. "This is a good meeting."

Jackie, ready to bolt and run at any moment, stopped as his friend started leading them to a row in front. As soon as Drew noticed that Jackie was no longer with him he turned around without a word and walked back. They sat in the last row.

Jackie looked around at a room he had never seen before. The folding chairs looked just as they did when it was used as a theater, but the people lined up in front of giant coffee-makers didn't look like an audience. The room was bigger, ominous, like an unexplored cave with demons lurking just overhead. The walls were papered with corny slogans. The smoke in the room was thick enough to choke even a chain-smoker like Jackie; smokier even than it was during his rehearsals. And his heart was pounding harder than it ever had in this room. Maybe harder than it ever had in any room.

It smelled of a drama he didn't want to share.

"This year's the Bicentennial, Jackie," Drew was saying. "Good year for independence."

"Jesus, Drew; don't get all metaphorical on me. I'm just here to look around."

He had trouble saying *metaphorical.* The drink he stopped off for hadn't worn off. Neither had the drinks he had at lunch.

"I don't want that kind of independence," he said. "I've seen too many reformed drunks in movies and television. All the sanctimonious whiners who've taken the cure. How come you're not like that?"

"First of all, we're not *reformed*, Jackie. Being a drunk driver's a crime; being a drunk isn't. And we're not *cured*, either. There isn't any cure. I'm still an alcoholic. I'll always be an alcoholic. I just don't drink. And I go to meetings. Beware of what you learn from movies and television. I don't know if you've ever noticed, but—they lie a lot."

Jackie was trying not to look directly at the others in the room; looking down quickly if eye-contact was made. He took a deep breath and held it a while.

"All right," he said, "I'll admit I'm in trouble. Now do I raise my hand and tell everybody I'm worthless?"

"Can't," Drew said. "You've been drinking today. That means keep quiet. People here like to say: *Take the cotton out of your ears and stuff it in your mouth.* Wait'll you've been sober all day—then talk.

"And, Jackie—you're not worthless."

Jackie was pretty sure he was. Twenty-four hours earlier he'd been in the Broadcast Grill in a heavy necking session with a woman he'd never seen before; a woman who was as drunk as he was. Forty years old and he was necking like an overheated high-school kid in a bar full of people who knew him and knew his wife. It was not something the real Jackie Barron did anymore. At least not in public. Except that tonight he *did* do it, and if some sonofabitch friend of theirs should tell his wife what happened ... God damn friends, anyway!

"I don't know if I can do this, Drew. Look at that sign about the 12 Steps. I can't even handle the first one. *Admitted we were powerless over alcohol?*"

Jackie, breathing faster, wondered if anyone else could hear the rattle that had settled between his throat and his chest.

"I'm not *powerless*, Drew. I just drink too much. I hate that word *powerless*."

"Doesn't mean *you're* powerless. You had the power to get yourself here, didn't you? Just means you're powerless over *alcohol*. Like everything else in life —it's all in where you put the emphasis."

The meeting began, and gradually Jackie forgot about Drew. He saw everything through a haze thicker than the smoke; heard everything through an echo-chamber; recognized his life being laid out by people he didn't know.

A young man spoke of having finally passed a whole day without once feeling ashamed or guilty. Jackie looked at the floor; he couldn't begin to imagine that.

A woman spoke of ninety days without a drink the way others might speak of a cancer in remission, and the room burst into applause. She got more applause than most of the plays he'd directed there.

A woman with a corrosively depressed lover said: "Sometimes I wish *she* was an alcoholic. Then I'd know how to help her." Everyone in the room seemed to understand and agree. Jackie thought it was insane.

A man smiled ruefully as he told horror stories of his contemptible moral failures and degradation—and the others in the room laughed. Gallows-humor, shared by survivors.

Jackie didn't laugh. He took a Kleenex out of his pocket.

During the beak in the proceedings the coffee he was carrying shook out of the paper cup and onto his fingers.

"How do you feel?" Drew said.

"*How*? Like I came from another planet, and I never knew it. Like I'm in a room full of people just like me for the first time. And I'm not breathing too good."

"Remember how we used to say *Let's go get drunk and BE somebody*? We always were somebody, Jackie."

"Yeah; maybe. I almost see that. But I don't know if I'll see that tomorrow. I don't know. A drunk is who I am, Drew. There are places where I'm famous: drink anyone under the table. Instant transformation; bland to brilliant. Why would anybody bother to know me if I'm not a colorful drunk anymore?"

"Don't worry about it," Drew said. "You'll still be a drunk. You'll just be a sober one."

Jackie didn't answer. The mystery was too much for him. The caffeinated strangers returning to their seats—his fellow alien life-forms?—were all too much for him.

But he appreciated an irony that he *could* find amusing. Before sitting back down he laughed aloud, because he found himself thinking how glad he was that those goddamn theater people hadn't been allowed to preempt this meeting for some stupid rehearsal.

New York, 1976

One Wrong Step

The Ninth Step was going to be a bitch; no question about that. There wasn't anything easy about getting sober, but some things were harder than other things. Telling his ex-wife about Elena was going to be the hardest of all.

No way around it. Alcoholics Anonymous was built on the twelve "Suggested Steps," and nowadays Jackie Barron was built on Alcoholics Anonymous. Nineteen-seventy-six had begun with his first reluctant appearance at an AA meeting; now, almost a year later, he was at a meeting every night, but he was no longer reluctant. No; he didn't feel he had a lot of choice in this matter. And taking the ninth Suggested Step meant making direct amends to the people you hurt when you were drunk. That would include pretty much everyone Jackie ever knew, but no one more than Lara Heller, who used to be Lara Heller Barron. By the time he had been 90 days sober and showed signs of maybe surviving in spite of himself, it was already too late. Lara had a divorce lawyer and an apartment of her own.

Still, the Ninth Step offered him a way to avoid the problem: You shouldn't do the "amends" with someone who would just be hurt all over again. Could Lara still be hurt? Who knew. They'd been divorced long enough for the shouting to be over, and if she got mad all over again—well, the dictionary defined amends as "payment made or satisfaction given," and she could probably find a world of satisfaction in getting furious and making him pay for it publicly.

Jackie looked up and watched the short, compact woman sweeping grandly through the door of the restaurant and descending on his table near the back. Lara Heller knew how to make an entrance.

"Club soda suits you, Jackie," she said. "Matches your complexion. You should have made the switch years ago." Lara wasn't big on "Hello-how-are-you." She just dropped her bag into an empty chair at the table and sat down.

"Thank you for coming, Lara."

"You said on the phone that this was going to be painful for you; how could I miss that?"

"And, gee, it's good to see you, too."

"My pleasure. I hope. While I'm enjoying your discomfort I might even slip up and get real for a minute-and- a-half and tell you I'm rooting for you. How long has it been?"

"I've been sober all day," Jackie said. "For a hundred and twenty-four days. But who's counting." The hundred-and-twenty-four days had actually taken a toll *off* Jackie's face. The dark circles under his eyes had faded and he was looking less than his forty-one years.

Lara didn't answer; she just stuck one hand straight up in the air and waved a languid wave to summon a waiter. Charlie's was a Times Square theater-bar owned by two guys named Charlie, and four in the afternoon was their empty time. Lara was a regular but she wasn't usually there at that time of day; the waiter didn't know her, so he hadn't hurried over.

Leaning over the table with her chin propped up on her hand, she gave Jackie a dangerously innocent gaze and said,

"So—how's Cassie Sullivan?"

Jackie allowed himself a sigh. "Peace, please?" he said. "Cassie has nothing to do with why we're here."

"Oh, good," Lara said. "How is she anyway? I like to keep track of people who've tried to poison my life."

Jackie, resigned, just shook his head. "According to her last letter she's fine, Lara. I can't swear to that because I haven't seen her for six or seven years."

"Oh, don't worry," she said. "You will. I read those hidden letters, remember? Put them all together, you could sell them to a porn magazine."

"You know the fantasies in those letters weren't real," he said, an edge creeping into his voice. "But they were fun. God knows you and I hadn't been for a long time."

"That's it," Lara said, reaching for her purse. "I'm gone."

"Wait. Please. You know we didn't get divorced because of Cassie or anyone else, Lara. We got divorced because of us."

Lara stopped, re-thought her exit, and leaned back into her chair.

"All right," she said. "Let's start the conversation all over again. I don't really care how Cassie Sullivan is—how are *you*? This is the first time I've actually seen you since you started stopping your love affair with Jack Daniel's. Should I have club soda too?"

"I would be mortified if you did," he said. "I'm just a drunk who's sober, not a born-again Pentecostal. But I did stay out of bars for ninety days, the way they tell you to, and I still don't go back to the old haunts —"

"Jackie, 'old haunts' for you means every bar on the West Side. I wouldn't –"

The waiter, finally arriving at the table, pointed towards the front of the room and said, "Charlie says hello." The Charlie named Dobson, trapped on the telephone, waved cheerfully at Lara. She threw him a kiss and turned back to the waiter. "Better make it a vodka stinger, rocks. I've been promised a bumpy afternoon."

When the waiter was gone, Jackie said, "I don't know, babe; maybe it won't be that bad. It's been a long time, and it's not something I would ever have talked about, but there's only one really ugly secret left that you didn't figure out years ago. You won't like it, but at least now you'll know it all. And know that I'm not just sorry now–I always was."

"Let's give ourselves a civilized pause before the drink gets here," she said. "I have no idea what you think you can tell me now that's going to be worse than what I've already survived. If you tell me you snuck in and poisoned my dog while I wasn't looking, that would be worse. Since he was busy tearing up the apartment when I left, that can't be it. Whatever it is, let's just wait until I'm fortified before you leap into today's melodrama. You never looked *this* funereal at funerals."

The air around the table had darkened. Lara Heller had brought a light mood in with her; her tongue could be sharp but her laughter was buoyant even when she was subdued, and her smile and a quip got her through painful moments. She seemed to realize that they weren't the right approach for this one, so she stopped trying.

They waited. The stinger came, and Jackie sat silently, watching the woman he'd loved and feared and pursued and dodged and tried not to feel inferior to through five tumultuous years. Everyone they knew had envied their perfect marriage, but the people they knew weren't there on the nights when Jackie and Lara were alone and the laughter degenerated into snarling. When they both finally realized that they didn't want to be there anymore either, divorce followed.

Lara leaned down and took a sip from the full-to-the-top drink to avoid lifting and spilling it. When she straightened up she took a deep breath and said, "So—if I'm just here so you can tell me you've gone running back to Cassandra Sullivan—don't bother. I could have told *you* that. Of course she's got her claws back into you. I'm surprised you didn't bring her with you."

"Lara, I told you a few thousand times—and I didn't ask you to come here just so I could tell you again—Cassie had nothing to do with anything. You and I got divorced because of me and you. Maybe mostly me, but you pushed."

Lara leaned over the table and gently patted the back of Jackie's hand.

"I didn't have to push, my darling. You started falling out of the marriage before the *I do's* dried."

"Lara—please let's don't let's do this again. I wasn't having an affair with Cassie or anyone else. We wrote letters, yes, but I haven't actually *seen* her for six or seven years. We're not here about things you *think* you know. We're here about things you're *entitled* to know. Okay?"

"Well, you were never a very good liar, so I'll take your word for it. Not that I give a damn. Let's just get this over with."

"Fine. When you were doing *Young and Rare...*" he said, and then fell silent.

Lara let the silence spread for an uncomfortable moment before saying "Okay; I'm following you so far. I did *Young and Rare.* Actually, I already knew that. I haven't been in so many hits that I can forget one. What about it?"

"There was a party at Donna Harris's house during your out-of-town tryouts. A lot of the old crowd from the Players Theater. It got pretty drunk out."

"Gee," she said. "Imagine that."

"Elena Hornak was there. You remember Elena."

"Of course I remember Elena. I despised her. She once told a director who didn't know me that I was very nice and wasn't it a shame about my weight problem."

Lara still didn't pick up her drink. Lara didn't move at all. She just looked Jackie directly in the eyes. Her own eyes said she saw the headlights that were coming at her.

"God damn you, Jackie. Even before you say whatever it is. God *damn* you."

"Just let me get through it, Lara. It's not easy."

"Oh, well; I certainly don't want to make anything *not easy* for you. I know how you hate *not easy*. Just get *on* with it!"

"Okay. We spent some time talking ... and she took me by the hand and we walked into Donna's back hall ... and the bathroom there was empty. Nobody was around, so we went in and locked the door."

Lara Heller still wasn't moving, but her breaths were coming slow and hard, "Go on," she finally said.

"Don't make me spell it out, Lara. You've got every right to be furious, but... Okay. Okay. I... had sex with Elena in the bathroom. It just happened."

Jackie stopped and laughed a nervous laugh in spite of himself. "If someone knocked on the door she'd stop... whatever we were doing... and say 'I'm in here! Come back later!' And then... go back to it."

"Oh, *thank* you for sharing that detail, Jackie! You're so *generous* in your storytelling! Didn't her mother teach her never to talk with her mouth full?" Lara's breaths were coming a lot faster now.

"I'm sorry. I'm *really* sorry. I ... anyway ... we didn't go back to the living room together. Hardly anybody even noticed we'd been gone."

"'Hardly anybody?' *Hardly* anybody? You screwed a vicious little tramp that I couldn't stand and then you say that maybe only a *few* people knew you'd banged her in the toilet? Which means that ten minutes later it damn well wasn't a secret to *anybody* but me? Those goddamn wannabe's never liked me to begin with; they must have had a *great* laugh about this!"

"Nobody *laughed*; for all I know nobody even *suspected* anything."

"*Shut up!*"

Lara's words had become so guttural Jackie half expected her to spit blood. She must have been feeling it herself, because she stopped for a deep breath. When she spoke again there was a deadly calm in the newly-measured flatness of her voice.

"You told me on the phone you were doing *amends* today. How the hell does this qualify as making *amends*? I swear to God, Jackie; I don't know whether you're confessing or bragging!"

"I've got nothing to brag about, Lara. It gets worse."

"What! You lying sonofa*bitch*, how much worse could it get? You told me there hadn't been anybody else; you *swore* there wasn't another woman!" The flatness was all gone.

To his own astonishment, Jackie became defensive. "Give me a break; there never was 'another woman'! This was one time in a toilet! And I was drunk."

"Oh, what the hell does *that* mean? You were always drunk! Now give me the rest of it. *What's worse*?"

Lara's rage was in her eyes and in the razor blades wrapped inside her words. Jackie broke eye-contact, glanced over her head, and saw her friend Charlie carefully not listening from his perch at the door.

"You remember when the tour was over and the show came into town?" he said. "You remember what happened?"

"Of course I remember. I thought I was going to get fired before we opened, and then they put in two new songs for me and we ran for nine months and three weeks. What do you mean *do I remember*?"

"Do you remember I told you I had... an intestinal problem? I didn't seem to be sick but I really was, and... and so I couldn't make love to you when you got home?"

"Jesus, Jackie; does *everything* have to be about you? You tell me about *adultery* and then you whine because you had a bellyache? I was disappointed, but I haven't been *brooding* over it all this time."

"I didn't have an intestinal problem, Lara! I had gonorrhea. I didn't dare touch you until the doctor guaranteed me it was cleared up."

The horror on Lara Heller's face had driven away every other expression. Even the rage seemed suspended for the moment. Her mouth hung open, but no words came. Jackie waited silently, the way a condemned man should.

"You. Disgusting. *Pig*." Lara spoke slowly and distinctly. "I needed you. The show was in trouble... I was hurting... I felt fat and ugly and *not good enough*! And you weren't there for me because you screwed Elena Hornak and got '*something awful in your belly*?' Well it wasn't awful enough!"

Lara's voice had come as near to a screech as she could allow herself. She didn't give a good goddamn who heard. Most of her drink was still in the glass when she picked it up, and then all of her drink was dripping down Jackie Barron's face. The one remaining ice-cube bounced off his forehead. He didn't reach up to wipe anything away.

"You are scum, Barron!" Now the control was back. Lara's voice was a flamethrower with a laser's precision. "You are scum and I hope the next scaggy bitch you climb up on gives you something that will rot your cock like a diseased fig!"

She had grabbed up her purse and was on her way to the door before she stopped, paused for a moment, then turned around and walked back to the table. Reaching out with her finger—Jackie resisted the temptation to dodge—

she scooped a drop of the stinger off his face, put it in her mouth, and sucked it gently before saying:

"I fucked the *Young and Rare* stage-manager when we played Boston." The defiance in her eyes matched her sneer.

Turning away like the dancer she once was, she threw her shoulders back, nodded to Charlie as she passed, and walked out with the dignity of a matador after the kill. Lara Heller also knew how to make an exit.

Jackie, sometimes unconsciously old-fashioned in his courtesies, had stood when Lara rose, but he didn't exit. He sat back down at the table, wondering why people actually believed that keeping secrets was a *bad* idea. Wondering who on earth first said confession is good for the soul. Wondering if his AA sponsor would be furious with him for this apparent mangling of the "amends" step. He wondered if he was even ready to stay sober.

Lara's vodka stinger had dripped down to his upper lip, but he carefully wiped the last drops away before he opened his mouth.

New York, 1980

The Bottom Line

"You're *what?*"

"Oh, for God's sake, Jackie; don't make such a big deal about it. I'm going to do one more film; that's all. I need the money. Atlantic City's just a maybe and some lounge off the Strip is the best my agent can do for me in Vegas. I bought that goddamn house on Fire Island and now I've got to pay for it. So don't yell at me!"

"I'm not yelling, Corinna. You're yelling. You're yelling because you goddamn know you're making a mistake. What the *hell* are you thinking?!"

"That was yelling! Don't tell me it wasn't yelling; Jackie; it was. You never took that tone with me before. Never!"

"Well, you never told me you were going to make another porn movie before, Corinna."

"*Adult films*, Jackie, they're called a*dult films*!"

"All right; call it whatever you want. The point is, you're trying to casually tell me you're going to do a butt-buster scene! Jesus Christ, woman—we were together for a year and a half and you never even let *me* in there!"

"Don't be disgusting, Jackie. That was different. And that's the only thing you ever wanted that I ever said no to. Isn't that true? Isn't it?"

"Yes, it's true, godammit! That's the whole point. I accepted that. We were terrific in bed and I could understand you being afraid of that one thing. Did I even argue with you? I did not. Did I *ever* give you grief about *anything*? I did not. No man exactly loves it that his girlfriend's art-form involves fucking for the camera, but I accepted it. *Didn't* I?"

"You accepted it because we were both too drunk to give a fuck about the fucking, Jackie. Do you think just because we're both sober now, that gives you a right to judge me? We haven't even been a couple for ten years! "

"I'm not sitting in fucking judgment, Corinna. I'm just trying to make you see what you're doing. And leave the sober shit out of the mix for once, okay? I'm not your sponsor and nobody's *making* you do this. You don't have to listen to me. Just listen to *yourself*, for chrissake"

"All right! I'm listening to myself and here's what I'm hearing: I'm hearing that I had the most famous butt in the business. I was the Jennifer Lopez of adult films when I retired. Well, it's five years later, and a lot of gym-time has kept that booty as bodacious as it was then. I'm hearing that Hindsight Films is offering me five figures for that one scene—one day's work, Jackie, probably just a couple of hours of *one day*. All I've got to do is let some overhung stud make Adult history popping into my bottom. So, yeah; I'm scared shitless—which, admit it, would be for the best in the situation—"

"Oh, don't make poop-jokes; this is not funny!"

"No, and you yelling doesn't make it funny either! Let me talk. Yes, I'm scared. Yes; I'm forty years old and I'm an anal virgin, but I'm also forty years old with a mortgage and no nightclub gigs until October. Other people do it that way all the time—how bad could it hurt? You telling me all gay guys are sado-masochists?"

"Okay, Corinna; okay. Let's look at it another way. You're into a new life. You're sober long enough to call yourself sober. You're out of the porn industry—call it whatever you want, it's still *porn*—you've been out long enough to get hired in respectable clubs that use your name to show how cool they are. When you took the most famous derriere in the business into retirement without passing it around you became a legend. You want to throw all that away? You retired with dignity, Corinna."

"*Dignity*? Jesus Christ, Jackie; I was a porn star. I fucked for a living."

"No. No, not really. Shall I remind you how you explained it to me when you first got *into* this 'adult' crap? You told me it was just *making movies* for a living. Maybe they involved fucking, you said, but they weren't the same as whoring. Not that there's anything wrong with whoring, if it's what you really want to do. But whoring wasn't what you wanted to do."

"Well, godammit, I wasn't! I was *acting*. Making movies was my *business*!"

"Well... you were a lousy business-woman. Once you were a big porn star, any good escort-service could have sold your sweet favors for a nightly fee a whole lot higher than what you were making. Still could. Maybe more *now* than *then*; there's a hell of a baby-boomer nostalgia-crowd out there."

"Goddamn you, Jackie, I am not a prostitute and I never was! You pointed that out to me yourself. You forget everything—did you forget what you said when you finally stopped trying to make me quit? I'll remind you—you didn't like it, but you said that it wasn't just that I had the best bottom in adult films. You said I was also the best actress. Okay, maybe except for Georgina Spelvin. She was our Meryl Streep. But except for her, I was the best. You knew what I did for a living when we met, and it didn't matter. We'd gone out three times before we ever went to bed. Do you remember *that*?"

"Of course I remember. And I told you I was a television PR guy, which meant I got called a whore more often than you did. And that didn't define me, so why would I think it defined you? I didn't like what you did, Corinna, you always knew that, but by God I loved the way you could be in that world without belonging to it. But that was *then*. This is now. You decided to get out, and you did. Remember when we met again at the AA meeting on 69th street? You told me there was nothing you were ashamed of. You were just proud that you never did anything you didn't want to."

"I always thought it was pretty funny that we got reunited on a street called 69."

"Oh, shut up, Corinna. We're talking serious here. Let's count it out. One: If you felt right about what you're about to do you wouldn't have called me, you'd have just done it. Two: Your inviolable ass is as famous in some circles as Betty Grable's legs or Streisand's nose. Do you think Streisand would get her nose done just to make a couple of mortgage payments? It's important to be known for some things you *won't* do, Corinna. Three: You haven't made a porn movie since you've been sober. You'd *hate* it now. You know you would. You're making a big mistake, baby. *Big* mistake. If anyone's going where no man's gone before, it should be someone who cares about you. You know that, too. That's why you called *me*. We haven't been a couple for a lot of years, girl. But you called *me*. Not your AA sponsor or your business manager. *Me*."

"All right! All *right*! Jesus Christ! I'll tell them no. I'll do a couple of weeks pole-dancing in Vegas and stall on the mortgage. But you are a bigger pain in the ass than that scene would have been, Jackie Barron!"

Corinna DeVegh slammed down the phone. Jackie Barron exhaled, smiled and spoke softly to the uninhabited line.

"*Accept the things I cannot change, courage to change the things I can and the wisdom to know the difference.*

"It's all about knowing the difference, babe."

New York, 1982

Ah Yes, I Don't Remember It Well

He had barely gotten past introducing himself—*My name is Jackie B and I'm an alcoholic* —when he spotted a familiar face in the second row. She obviously recognized him, too. Trying to ignore her, he began his story, starting with an overview of his drinking days—about 4,000 of them by his rough count.

What he was thinking was: *Good God—I know that woman. I wonder who she is.*

Aloud, he was telling the room about his first drink, at a party in high school. It was vodka and orange juice; teenagers in the '50s were convinced that vodka was undetectable by parents.

"I was seventeen, and when I stumbled out of that party—I fell down once, but very gracefully—I knew I'd found the solution to everything wrong in my life. Vodka and orange juice were going to make me witty, charming, and irresistible to girls. I even vomited in a charming and witty way that night," he said.

While the rest of the recovering alcoholics in the room laughed—they'd all believed the same damn-fool things at one time or another—Jackie checked out the woman in the second row again.

Why do I know her? Good-looking woman. I never forget a good-looking woman. Maybe she'll stand up when I'm finished and say "I'm... Somebody-or-other... and I'm an alcoholic."

But which *fucking alcoholic?*

Had to happen. He'd shared a drink or twenty with a lot of women; one of them was bound to be in a 12-step program by this time. A lot of them probably should be. Most of them probably should be. So she was somebody he drank with.

Okay; it's happened. I'll think of her name. Please, God, don't let her be somebody I was a shit to.

Finally, while his story was in college, where he had a best friend who could buy beer because he had a fake ID that made him twenty-one, Jackie got it. No good reason—he just got it. Her name was *Lauren.* Lauren something. She'd been one of his contacts when she was working for TV Guide. Of course he remembered her. But they hadn't ever *done it.* Had they?

He remembered setting up the last interview she did before she quit the job and disappeared. And after the interview that night, they... *what*?

Jackie pulled his thoughts together and tried to consign the mystery to a back corner. He was getting to the tough part of his story. The wife who put up with him longer than she should have before she left him. The job he'd almost lost because his bosses weren't sure they could trust him not to get drunk and embarrass the network. The women he'd loved and driven away, usually taking some really nasty memories with them.

Did I sleep with her? he wondered. He wasn't partial to euphemisms, but he wasn't comfortable just asking himself: *Did I fuck her?* After all, he barely knew her.

Finally, he was summing up his story. Signaling Lauren-something with a smile. Acknowledging the uneasy smile she flashed back. His said, "Of course I remember you. Stay right there." Hers answered, "Good. I'm here." He wondered if she was as uneasy about this as he was.

The group applauded—nothing like a tale of degradation and survival to get a round of applause from people who've been there, done that. The secretary called for the break; people moved towards the coffee-pot and Jackie headed straight for the second row.

"Hey, Lauren," he said, putting his arms around her. "Do I say *I'm happy to see you here*? Or do I say, *Oh—I'm so sorry to see you here*?"

Lauren put her arms around him. Sober alcoholic meetings were like that. "Both, I hope. I'm sorry either of us has to be here. But thank God we made it, right?"

"That is correct! Lauren has answered our first Meaningful Question in the absolute properest of manners!" Jackie stepped back and took her hands. "But Jackie Barron tops her: (1) - Lauren *Caruthers*. (2) - TV Guide. (3) - Missing since... Summer 1968. Fourteen years. Right?"

"You're a winner, Jackie. Always were."

"Ah, Lauren," he said, grinning and squeezing her fingers. "Out of all the recovering-from-gin joints in all the world, you had to walk into mine."

"And I'm glad I did," she said. "I live downtown so I never get to meetings up here. It was weird when you started talking and I thought *Omygod! I know that guy!*"

Lauren was smiling. In spite of the maddening uncertainty, it really was like running into an old friend. "The last time I saw you was the Maureen Shea interview in the Oak Room at the Plaza," she said. "See? My brain didn't *completely* calcify".

'Last time' I saw you was at the Oak Room...? he thought *Well... not exactly.*

"What I *couldn't* remember," she said, "is if I did anything to you I should apologize for. I *think* I know. I think I didn't. Did I?"

Jackie put a hand on her shoulder and they walked to a part of the room that was mostly deserted because it was away from the coffee-pot. They turned two chairs around so they could sit facing each other.

"I'm not exactly a monument to memory skills, Lauren, but I can *definitely* say you have nothing to apologize for. I even remember the story you wrote about Maureen after the interview. Considering the flow of drinks across that table I was amazed you could write anything. You were really good."

Jackie tried not to wonder if "really good" sounded like a subtle sexual comment. *Nah. She knows that's not my style. Or maybe it was back then. Or did she even notice?*

The blush on Lauren's cheeks suggested that she was wondering the same thing. "Good. Thank you," she said. "I didn't think I did anything ugly."

And then she shook her head, waved her hand in front of her face as though she were dismissing a fog, and said, "Oh, what the hell. You probably already know what's bothering me.

"What I don't know exactly," she said, "is what happened after we left Maureen Shea at the Plaza. I wish I could say it's because my memory is failing, but I remember not being sure the next morning, either."

"Oh," he said. "Well... blackouts are God's way of telling us there are some things we're not meant to know. If we beat ourselves up over everything we couldn't remember we'd spend our whole lives with broken cheekbones, wouldn't we?"

There was no one very near them in the church basement, but Lauren leaned in and spoke a little softer. "No, really. Let's talk about this for a minute. I know we went back to my place. I remember clearing everything off the sofa and pouring a few drinks."

"Jack Daniel's," he said. "Or cooking sherry. I didn't discriminate in those days."

"We traded some stories—I sorta remember crying at some point—and I think maybe we kissed—a lot," she said. "My skirt probably wound up pretty high on my thighs ... and the screen fades to black. That used to happen a lot in those days. I'm sure you didn't stay the night. I think I'd remember that."

"Lauren; it was a long time ago and —"

"I know," she said. "It's okay. Embarrassing but okay. It's just that seeing you brings it all back. *Part* of it all back. And I really do have something to apologize for. I remember getting the messages that you called. I wasn't returning anybody's calls, Jackie. Everything bad was getting worse. I'd been drinking my lunches, missing deadlines. I was having a lot of sex-on-the-first-dates—and sometimes I didn't wait that long. I remembered all that; I just didn't want to."

She held for a moment to see if that last image would inspire a response. It didn't.

"I quit the job—they were going to fire me anyway—and I went home to Anaheim. Hid out in my mother's house like some crazy lady. She kept reminding me I was thirty years old and still not married. I told her I just hadn't met the right guy yet. But I wasn't really sure that was true.

"I met a lot of right guys," she said. "Probably including you. They just weren't right for *me*. I always thought I was a perfectly normal, small-town California girl, but it wasn't working. When I started going to AA meetings I felt like saying 'My name is Lauren C and I don't know *what* the hell I am. What's *wrong* with me!'"

Jackie continued to sit in silence.

"Here comes the dramatic revelation," she said. "I finally discovered what it was. I couldn't find the right guy because the right guy was a girl."

Now Jackie reacted. He didn't say anything, but he reacted.

"Thank you for looking surprised," she said. "I'd hate to think I was the only one who didn't know. I met Susan in one of these meetings after I came back to New York. She was very principled about no romantic involvements during my first year sober, but the day it was over—we were lovers. And nine years later we still are.

"So it turned out I was a perfectly normal, small-town California lesbian. And there wasn't anything wrong with me at all."

"That's great, Lauren," Jackie said, mostly meaning it. "It really is. How're you doing now?"

"I'm doing good, Jackie. If Susan and I ever come to this meeting together you'll meet her. That'll be interesting. She knows I wasn't a virgin, but she's never met any man I was involved with. She tends to be a little sensitive about my past, so if you do meet her..." She stopped. Jackie was actually blushing.

"I barely knew ya," he said. "You were just another pretty reporter trying to pick my brains for swell gossip. Besides which ..."

He was looking her pointedly in the eyes and shaking his head slowly.

"We didn't?" she said.

Jackie's head kept moving from side to side.

"We did?"

Jackie took her hands again.

"You're fishing in a dry well," he said.

It was Lauren's turn to react.

"Are you saying ...?"

Jackie spread his hands, palms up, and shrugged his shoulders.

Lauren's grin was radiant. "No, you're *not* saying! You're not saying anything. *You don't know what happened either,* do you! You blacked out the same as I did! You don't know!"

Now Jackie nodded, trying not to look as sheepish as he felt.

"Well... well, good," she said. "Trust me—I am not offended. A drunken straight guy bedding a drunken lesbian probably wouldn't have involved a lot of moments to be treasured, anyway."

"Then let's pretend that we both think that," Jackie said. "Even if it's not really true. I think *I* don't want to remember because I don't want to think about what I might have missed. I'm still stuck at your skirt sliding up your legs."

"Ah, Jackie, you always did put a *saucy* edge on things," Lauren said. "We can just share an appreciation for the bright side of blackouts. And if you meet Susan, we won't have anything to hide.

"Can't talk about things we don't know, can we?"

New York, 1983

Meeting Deborah

Winding up in bed with Deborah Simon came as a surprise but not a shock.

Jackie Barron had known her for more than twenty years and he had always found her sexy as hell, but—except for that one time eight or ten years ago when they rolled around on the floor, both too drunk to do much more than that—their friendship had never been physical. She said he was the brother she never had.

By 1975 she had worked her way up to her fourth—fifth?—unsuccessful suicide attempt, only two of which were serious enough to take her to Bellevue. Jackie had ridden in the ambulance with her both times.

A few years and many lovers later, she had moved to Lenox, Massachusetts, with her third—fourth?—husband who didn't last long.

Over the years, Jackie had learned to let the answering machine take her middle-of-the-night calls. Her voice was always slurred and he would eventually turn off the volume on the machine, because her endlessly wandering messages would continue even after the tape ran out. A call from Debbie Simon meant trouble, even at long-distance.

Still, he had heard recently from another friend that she was sober, that she'd given up the pills, that she had gotten her life semi-straightened out and was teaching Contemporary Poetry at a private school in Lenox. Today, she had called at three in the afternoon, rather than three in the morning. She said she was in town, and asked—

calmly and rationally—if she could spend the night on his couch. He interrupted the answering machine and picked up.

"Can I stay there tonight?" she said, as though there had never been a silence between them. "I'm not crazy and I'm not drunk and I'm going to stay at Bruce's—you do remember Bruce? Your godson? I'm staying with him for a week, but he doesn't get home until tomorrow, and he still doesn't like me to stay in his apartment when he's not there. It's just for the one night, okay?"

Debbie wouldn't be the first sexy woman who had ever slept chastely on his couch—he always had fantasies that one of his guests would creep silently into his bed in the middle of the night, but no one ever did—and he hadn't ever really *disliked* Debbie. He had just become exhausted by and fed up with sharing her melodramas. Since he'd gotten sober himself he had cut her out of his life in self-defense.

When he opened the door to her he noticed first that she looked terrific. Her eyes were clear, even looking happy to see him. Her hair, cropped to her head like a helmet, was professionally red but the freckles sprinkled across her nose were real. He felt a rush remembering what never was.

He picked up her suitcase, carried it inside and set it down, took her in his arms, and kissed her nicely. Her breath was sweet, which hadn't always been the case. And the nice-to-see-you kiss seemed a little sweeter than he remembered.

"It's good to see you, Debbie," he said. "Especially looking like this. Good looks may be superficial but they're *good.*"

"Stop right there," she said. "*Debbie's* a cheerleader's name. I'm forty-five years old and I've got three grown sons, for God's sake; it's time to be *Deborah.* Okay?"

It was 1983 and Jackie had known her since 1960—before she started lying about her age. He was forty-eight now, so she had to be fifty+, but what the hell. In this world you were only as old as you looked.

"I'll try to remember," he said. "Kissing you was a feast when I thought you were Debbie; let's see how Deborah tastes."

The taste of Deborah was lovely, and the deeper he went the lovelier it got. When he broke away and looked at her eyes, they both knew where this was going, so they went.

In the bedroom, Jackie undressed her slowly. He had never seen her naked—that time on the floor didn't get anywhere near that state—and the shape of her breasts was all he could have asked, which was also true of her belly, her hips and her thighs. Perhaps her knees were a little knobby, and her calves a trifle thin, but so were his.

Still fully dressed himself, Jackie sat her on the bed, kissed her and dropped to his knees on the floor in front of her. He traveled slowly up this unexplored body, letting his lips do the walking. It was a lovely trip.

"Get naked, Br'er Jackie," she said when he finally reached the lobe of her left ear. "I want to watch."

Jackie found it difficult to imagine anybody wanting to watch *him* undress, but he did so, and she seemed to like what she saw.

When his belt-buckle hit the floor he returned to Debbie—Deborah—joining her on the bed, returning to the junction of her thighs. The taste that met his tongue was different from the taste of her lips but no less welcome. When she said *AhhhAHHH!!* he decided to explore that neighborhood further.

Eventually he moved back up until they lay side by side, and then she was under him and more than his tongue was inside her. Punctuating the words with the thrust of his hips, he said "I've wanted ... to do this... *forever*. But right now... I'm glad it's happening... right *now*." Breathless exclamation points punctuated Deborah's repeated *Yes! Yes! Yes!*

When her *Yes!* changed to *Oh, God! Oh, God!* Jackie rolled onto his back without disconnecting. She was atop him now, and he was sure the neighbor could hear her through the wall. He certainly hoped so.

Things continued like that for a long time. He had no idea how long, but he hoped it was *very* long. When they were lying side by side again he gently guided her onto her stomach so he could pay his respects to the rest of her. She welcomed him.

After they both seemed incapable of even the tenderest movement, they lay close and quiet for a long time. Jackie glowed and then he dozed and when he awoke Deborah Simon was sitting beside him on the edge of the bed. She was still naked, but now she held a tall scotch in one hand—Jackie always kept a bottle around for guests—

and a cigarette in the other. When she leaned over to kiss him the taste was different, and so were her eyes—more familiar, more like the bad old days—and he flinched. Meeting Deborah had been an unqualified joy, but Debbie was still in there.

Sometimes, he thought, friends should just stay friends, but he didn't say that. He returned the kiss in silence, and wondered how serious a mistake they had made. And how long they could continue making it.

Pennsylvania, 1987

Alisa

Alisa Danilova was 75, beautiful, and dying.

Jackie Barron—who was 23 years younger—knew how old she was because she had told him, when they first became lovers, that she had cut six years off her life by altering the date of birth from 1912 to 1918 on her passport. ("I'd have made it 1928," she said, "if I thought I could get away with it.")

She was beautiful in a way that Jackie loved. She once described her body as "just your basic Russian peasant," to which Jackie had replied, "If every little peasant girl in Russia walks around with legs and a bottom like yours, it's no wonder every man in Dostoyevsky gets crazy."

She was dying because she'd been a heavy smoker all her life.

In the dimly lit room, Jackie concentrated on her eyes. Even with the little plastic tubes feeding her pure oxygen, the beauty was there. The cancer hadn't done as much damage to her face as he'd feared. Her cheekbones had always been remarkable. The loss of weight had only exaggerated them.

"How on earth did you get here?" she asked. "How did you even know *I* was here?"

"Your sister called me. I was surprised. I didn't think she ever really approved of me."

"Of course she didn't. She called you my *middle-aged fancy-man.*"

Alisa had been his editor when he was free-lancing magazine stories, and they were friends who flirted, nothing more. She'd been retired for six years before the friendship heated up one night and eventually exploded them into her bedroom.

Months later, when she moved out of the city and back to Pennsylvania, she had said "Mr. Cole Porter described us, Jackie. Too hot not to cool down."

Now, she just said, "It's lovely to see you, Jackie. I'm not so sure I'm happy about *you* seeing *me*. Not like this."

Jackie put his hand on the cheek that had been full and smooth. It was stretched loosely on the planes of her face now, but it still felt good under his palm.

"There isn't an inch of you that I haven't committed to memory," he said. "You know I used to undress you with my eyes when we worked together. Well, now I'm stripping away the sheet and the blanket with my mind—and it's still you under there."

Laughing no longer came easy for Alisa, but her lips and her eyes provided the hoped-for reaction.

"You are a dreadful person, Jackie Barron. And I miss that. They're very nice to me here. But no one is likely to tell me I have a '*memorable derrière.*' Or applaud my *knees*, for God's sake. I always loved it that you watched me pull on my stockings in the morning. Even though I'd been lying there naked next to you all night."

"That's because you never stopped exciting me, Alisa. Never," he said. "Is it bizarre that we're talking like this in your hospital room?"

"It's not a hospital, Jackie. It's a hospice. Big difference. What you mean is... while I'm on my dying bed. Don't wince like that—it's okay for me to say it. But I'd just as soon *you* don't."

Trying hard to follow her lead in this reunion, Jackie said, "What's the doctor telling you?"

"He's telling me that lung cancer doesn't fool around. And they found mine late. I have three to six months, Jackie. Non-negotiable."

"Is it... idiotic to ask how you feel about that?"

"Yes, it is, but it's okay. I'm scared to death. But I'm getting better about it. Drugs keep the pain in check. Most of the time. So let's not talk about that any more."

This time Jackie reached down and took her hands. The bones seemed to be fighting their way out. She couldn't miss the look of shock that he tried to submerge.

"Don't hold my hands, Jackie. They're awful. Let's talk about you."

So they did. He sat in the bedside chair and brought her up to date on people they knew in common, especially the impossible man who replaced her and edited Jackie to the point where he refused to write for them anymore. The magazine had lasted less than a year without her.

When he paused for a breath Alisa looked at him very directly and said, "I didn't leave New York because of you, you know. Not *only* because of you. Actually, I'd been *staying* because of you. I was 72 years old and I *liked* being a sexy lady in your eyes. I didn't really expect that to happen again."

"I didn't expect it ever to stop," he said.

"Oh, of course you did. I always knew it was insane to allow a few great nights to grow into an affair. And you knew it, too. But it was worth it."

Her smile was a little wider this time, as she said, with mock solemnity, "Adjusting to you sexually was the hard part, Jackie. I was *shocked.* I always thought the exciting older woman was supposed to teach her young lover the new tricks."

"Your *young lover* was 48 at the time, Alisa. And we both had to make some sexual adjustments. I'd never been with a woman so... let's say... *elegantly conservative...* as you. I was afraid you'd throw me out and get a restraining order."

"*That* was never a consideration," she said. "Everything that shocked me turned out to be very wonderful—or at least bearable—in the end —"

She stopped, and probably blushed—it was hard to tell. "And do *not* make a saucy joke about being in my *end*, because you *weren't.* It's fine that you were a vulgarian in bed, but this is a hospice and you should behave yourself. We don't want to get me all excited, do we? A person in my condition could die from a thing like that. Of course, that might not be such a bad way to go."

This time the smile was wide enough that it was probably hurting her a little. She didn't seem to mind.

"I will behave," he said. "But is it all right if I just *think* lewd and lascivious?"

"I couldn't bear it if you stopped. I'd think I was already dead."

Jackie risked an abrupt return to the subject.

"Why *did* you leave, Alisa?"

"Well, I didn't leave *just* because we were running down. I wasn't about to tell *you*, but I knew I'd be a burden in the not so distant future. Can you see yourself playing nursemaid? I couldn't. Besides, you'd have ended it yourself in another month or so. When you didn't make much effort to stop me, I got the signal.

"But it's all right," she said. "You know how people like to remember the wonder of their first affair? I wanted to remember the wonder of my last one. So, here are my final words of wisdom for you: If you know an ending is coming, always be the one who leaves... before it all falls apart."

Her smile was softer now. Her eyes were far away. He wanted to bend down and take her in his arms, but the whole machinery of medical science stood in the way.

They talked for a few minutes more, but the nurse who'd been nodding-in was becoming more persistent. It was time for him to leave.

"As long as there's a bus between New York and here, I'll be back, Alisa."

"Well. We'll see. If you do come... would you bring me something?"

"Of course."

"Do you still have those Polaroids?"

It was Jackie's turn to feel like blushing.

"You *know* I do."

"If you come again... bring me one to tuck under my pillow. My sister will probably have a heart attack if she finds it after I die. But I'll risk it. I'd much rather remember us that way than this."

"Me, too," he said. "Me, too."

New York, 1986

The Truth, A Little Truth, And Anything But

When the phone rang at eight o'clock that evening it came at a time in Jackie Barron's life when the craziness had definitely subsided. There wasn't a reason in the world for him to think he might regret it, so he answered on the first ring.

He regretted it.

The caller was Deborah Simon, and her opening words were, "Don't hang up, Jackie! Please. It's okay—I swear. I've been sober almost a year and I'm practically engaged and it's really good this time. Okay? I'm not Crazy Debbie anymore, remember?"

It was the sanest and soberest he had heard her in years. Maybe she had changed. Maybe.

She went directly to the point. Her almost-fiancée wanted to meet some of her friends, and Jackie was the only one she felt she could trust with him. So, please, could he join them for dinner... and could Jackie please not share any colorful stories from the old days, since she had maybe... *softened* things a little when she talked about her past.

Jackie figured he was making a mistake, but he'd made worse. "Of course," he said. "I'm happy for you." He'd known Deborah for twenty-five years—ever since she was still Debbie—and their relationship had gone through kaleidoscopic changes.

Now it was Friday night and he was at Deborah's apartment. Her complexion was clear, her eyes were full of hope, and her smile seemed happy; not manic. Her hair was short and natural; the gray was being allowed its rightful place.

Deborah looked good.

Seamus Hogan was the maybe-fiancée. He was big and loud, somewhere around forty (Deborah was fifty-something but denied it), and very Irish. He owned a livery cab and had met her one night when she was a passenger. People tended to warm up to Deborah quickly.

There were no cocktails before dinner—she was serious about her new life and Jackie had ten years sober. Seamus had a glass of wine and explained quickly that it was okay; Deborah said it didn't bother her.

"So you guys have known each other since the 60s?" Seamus said.

"All of the 60s," Jackie said. "A mutual friend introduced us." (Debbie had been sleeping with and madly in love with his oldest friend.)

"I guess you've been through a lot together," Seamus said. "She told me about how you came and bailed her out when she got arrested in that Civil Rights demonstration."

Oh, yes, Jackie thought. Only it had nothing to do with Civil Rights. And he couldn't bail her out because she was doing time for smuggling two pounds of marijuana into the country. He and Nick Christoforos, both short of cash as usual, had taken her a carton of cigarettes and a paperback collection of Dylan Thomas poems.

"That's right," he said. "She was the princess of her cell block. Getting arrested was a badge of honor in those days."

Deborah was serving what he knew was going to be a splendid dinner—even at her wildest, she never failed to be an angel in the kitchen. Her eyes caught his and said *thank you.*

"How about when she was working with abused women at Bellevue," Seamus said. "Did you know her then?"

Yeah, Jackie thought, *I knew her in the Bellevue days. Even went with her. Twice. In an ambulance holding her hand. When Debbie attempted suicide she always did it clumsily and phoned a friend–like me–while there was adequate time to get there.*

"Oh, yeah," he said. "I guess she's told you; she'd been through some rough patches herself. I think the women there knew she understood them."

"You make it sound like I just tell you about the dark side, Seamus," she said. "Don't forget, we also knew the nightlife in New York better than anybody since the Roaring Twenties. Didn't we, Jackie?"

Right. Jackie remembered the nightlife. Like the Britannia Cafe, a Greek belly-dancing palace on Eighth Avenue in Chelsea. Debbie loved it there. The last time they went–she had a mildly wealthy husband at the time, but he never accompanied them– she took Jackie and five or six others as her guests. Somewhere near closing time, in the rapture of the bouzouki music, she joined the dancers on the floor and pulled off her blouse, baring her pulsating belly (and the bra she had carefully kept on). Everybody cheered. When the manager interrupted and escorted her back to the table, she ordered champagne for everyone, and he invented a rule that champagne had to be paid for when ordered. When he came back he said "I'm sorry, Mrs. Simon, but the Diners Club instructed me to chop up your card and throw it away." She had to wake her husband to come and pay the bill they had already run up.

"No question about it," Jackie said. "Deborah put *life* into the night."

Over dessert—a perfect *crème brûlée*—Seamus lifted his glass in a toast. "She calls you the brother she never had, and I can see why."

Uh huh, Jackie thought. *He remembered the night three years ago, when they went from friends to lovers. At one point she shouted, "This is beautiful —I can fuck my brother and it isn't incest!"*

"I always appreciated that," Jackie said. "I *have* a sister, but with Deborah it was... *different.*"

When he thought he could do it gracefully, Jackie excused himself, first agreeing that they must do this again soon and he mustn't be a stranger. Seamus shook his hand warmly—inadvertently crushing the knuckles a little—and said how much he appreciated the way Jackie had filled him in on the Deborah he hadn't known.

As Jackie walked to the subway, he thought:

Maybe it'll last this time. You don't know. Maybe she'll surprise me.

He tried very hard not to think: *There's probably cold days in Hell. It could happen.*

New York, 1982

Last Call

McGovern's Tavern, on Columbus Avenue in New York City, was a treasure chest of firsts and lasts, although those treasures sometimes turned out to be fool's gold.

Jackie Barron became a regular at McGovern's with his first visit, in 1962. The place affected people that way. Twenty years later he was still a regular, even though he'd been a sober, seltzer-regular for the past six years.

He'd experienced a lot of first and lasts here—with the pleasurable outweighing the pitiful—and he remembered every one of them. Well, maybe not every one. But a lot. And, with the bar closing permanently at the close of this evening, the room was shoulder-to-shoulder with people sharing remembrances, many of them true.

Paddy himself was not a participant in the memory-lane strolls. He was the most practical of transplanted leprechauns, and nostalgia was not one of his vices. At four a.m. he would lock the door for the last time and walk away without a tear. It was time.

Nobody could tell for sure if Paddy was happy or sad about his retirement from the saloon he had owned for forty years

He was eighty or thereabouts—no one really knew—and he had owned and operated this watering hole ever since he came to America, holding court from his stool at the end of the bar. Nobody was surprised at not knowing how he felt, because that was Paddy's way: he knew everybody's secrets, but nobody knew his.

The regulars didn't share the saloonkeeper's disdain for *do-you-remembers?* Most of them worked in the News department at the Indie Broadcasting Network, which was headquartered right across the street, and they loved sharing stories—often the same stories they had already shared twelve times.

Doyle Garvin, for instance, was telling anyone who would listen about the weekend John Kennedy was shot. "We were sending every correspondent we could find to Dallas or Washington, and some to Hyannis Port, and in those days not everybody had a credit card. By the time we could get organized the banks were closed, and the network actually ran out of cash for travel expenses. I sent our business manager over here, and Paddy went to that safe in the back that we're not supposed to know about—"

McGovern interrupted him to say, "That particular pot of gold is empty tonight, so don't get any ideas."

"Paddy went back to the safe and pulled out $20,000 in cash," Gavin said, "which got us through the weekend. Monday morning somebody from Accounts Payable came over and repaid the money."

"And never a nickel in interest," McGovern added. "You're a cheap lot, you news people."

Don Jameson, a director who once spent Election night stretched out on tables pushed together in the back of the saloon, was telling a different financial story.

"Paddy never loaned *me* $20,000," he said, "but I could always keep a cab waiting while I ran in here to borrow $50 or so. You could trace my whole financial history just by looking at the big red ledger book behind the bar."

Almost no one in the room was surprised by that, because almost everyone in the room had been bailed out of one jam or another that same way.

Jackie Barron's mind was still caught up in beginnings and ends, and he thought back on his first drink here—a Jameson's neat, at Paddy's insistence. That first drink hadn't seemed particularly memorable; not like the last one.

"Did I ever tell you I came in here on my way to my first AA meeting," he asked McGovern. "I had a Johnnie Walker Black on the rocks that time—a double, I think—and then I went around to the basement of St. Stephen's."

"He was a good man, St. Stephen," McGovern said. "The only saint I know of who got rewarded for getting stoned. He's been watching over drunks ever since."

Jackie let that go by. "That was my last drink," he said. "My last *deliberate* drink, anyway. I had four martinis at lunch a week later. I was celebrating the wisdom I'd picked up at AA."

"I'm not an expert on Alcoholics Anonymous," McGovern said, "although God knows I've done my part to keep their membership growing—but I don't think that particular ritual is recommended to mark your first week."

"Yeah; I learned that the hard way. I even stayed out of here for the next ninety days."

"And everyone asked about you every one of those days," McGovern said. "My income took a thirty percent drop, and when the bartender looked at his tips every night he wept."

"It was never my intent to bankrupt you, Paddy. I figure I've been making up for it ever since by paying $1.50 for every five-cent glass of seltzer off the tap."

"I wouldn't have it any other way," McGovern said. "We even throw in a lime-slice on the house, just to show our appreciation."

"It won't be the same somewhere else," Jackie said. "I brought Cassie Sullivan here on our first date, and we went straight from here to my place. In between breakups with Cassie I brought Patty Mackenzie here. At the end she figured it would be a kindness to me if we came here for our last night together. She'd decided she might want to marry somebody someday, and that somebody wasn't likely to be me."

"You've known beautiful women, Jackie; you just don't seem able to keep hold of them. How many first dates have you *had* in here?"

"Most of them, Paddy, most of them. But we didn't end too many here. Although, now that I think of it, Cassie met me here the last time I saw her before she married and moved to New Mexico. That may be one last time too many."

The conversation was becoming depressingly gloomy, and the host had to pay a little attention to his other closing-night guests, so he took Jackie by the shoulders before moving away to charm the rest of the room.

"You ought to be used to it by now," Paddy McGovern said. "Think of it the way I do: every first time's got a last time built into it. It's a package deal. That won't cheer you up any, but ancient Irish wisdom rarely does."

It was the last time Jackie Barron saw Paddy McGovern, who had been much closer to death than anyone knew.

And Jackie chose never to have a first time to set foot inside the Starbucks that eventually replaced the sacred temple that had been McGovern's Tavern.

New York, 1985

The Jackie & Pattymac Reunion

When Patricia MacKenzie and Jackie Barron split in 1979 neither was the villain. Clean break. No regrets, no recriminations.

Six years later, sitting with her at an outdoor café table on Columbus Avenue in Manhattan, Jackie still marveled at the memory. Together for the first time since she moved to North Carolina, there were still no regrets except maybe a few.

Patricia, at forty-something, was looking great, but she always did. Her hair was still a long mass of reddish-brown curls; the reddish part was new. Her cheekbones were sculpted, her eyes were large and direct, her lips were wide and full and softly shining with a hint of lipstick. It was those lips that his eyes always returned to—then and now.

He wondered what she saw when she looked at his fifty-year-old self. He knew that a little more hair fell away with each shampooing, he knew the gray was creeping into what remained, and he knew about the little belly that had begun to resist his belt.

In spite of what he knew—and provided he wasn't looking at a photograph taken in an unforgiving light—he continued to see himself as he was at thirty. He doubted that she did.

They had stayed in touch through Christmas letters and the occasional phone call since she made the move. That couldn't cover everything, so on this sunny afternoon they had gone through all the what's-new details while they ate. Patricia was the primary still-photographer at the Wilmington film studio known as "Hollywood East," and a major gallery showing of her nature-photography had just opened. Jackie had added some new colorful stories—Patricia loved colorful stories—about working in Paris on a miniseries.

Now their meal was calling them back to memories of things past.

"I can't believe you're still eating all that fat," Patricia said, wincing at the sight of his cheeseburger. "I remember you worked your way up to my soy-bean chili. That was progress. But I also remember you would never eat my tofu."

"Whoa whoa whoa! That is *criminally* unfair! I got my face right in there and ate your tofu with enthusiasm, longevity and joy! What I *didn't* do is call it your '*tofu*'. When I use euphemisms they come from Chaucer, not some Yuppie cookbook."

"Ho ho," she said. "It's nice to see you haven't changed—you're still a pig. Which is good. Your dirty little mind was one of your most appealing traits."

"My mind has not bathed in four years," he said. "I can still talk the talk. And I would love to put that thought into action."

"Oh, behave! If I could photograph the inside of your head I'd have a gallery showing weirder than Helmut Newton. How about if we just talk like grownups for a change?"

"I think we used to spend too much time talking like grownups," Jackie said. "Loving me for my mind was the one cliché thing you ever did. Every woman who ever paid any attention to me said she was attracted to me for my mind. I went to a high school reunion once and a girl I worshipped in those days said, 'Of course I remember you. You were the smart one.' Do you have any idea how degrading that is? I saw me as a wild, wanton, mindless instrument of pleasure."

He assumed an appropriately glum expression and shook his head. "Never understood why nobody else could see that."

"If we can change the subject for a moment, Mr. Smut-Filth, I wanted to tell you that the picture of you trying to catch a fish in Providence is in my gallery showing. Want to come to Wilmington and see yourself? You can stay with me."

"What—and share a bed like a non-incestuous brother and sister again, like in Bang'er, Maine? I still can't believe I slept with a beautiful woman in *Bang'er* and didn't."

"It's BANG-gore, Jackie."

"I know. It just sounds like more fun my way. When I look back—and I do, you know—I think it's nice we traveled together after we split up. The only thing perverted was letting you talk me into fishing. I'd never touched a fishing rod in my life, and I liked it that way. I look like a silent-comedy reject in that picture."

"No, you don't. You look a little goofy but very sweet. In a piggy way, of course."

There was another silence, but the silences weren't awkward. They'd spent a lot of time sitting quietly when they were together. Then Jackie leaned over the table and spoke softly.

"You know, Pattymac, that ostentatiously good behavior was not because I've ever stopped seeing you as a sex goddess. Like now, for instance. Let's just say, hypothetically, that you're not involved with anybody—which you're not. And I'm not involved with anybody—which I'm not. And you'll be going back to Wilmington tomorrow—which you are. How about if I accidentally drop something under the table, and while I'm down there searching for it..."

"Stop it! Ostentatiously *bad* behavior won't get you anywhere, either." Patricia shook her head slowly and reached across the table, taking both his hands. "We've got a good arm's-length relationship, Jackie. Let's not screw it up by screwing."

"Okay. You're right. We ended good. We should probably leave it alone. Whether I like it or not. But can we still do stuff in my fantasies?"

Patricia sighed in resignation, but a grin was struggling to get out.

"Absolutely—at least until I get engaged to somebody. If and when. In your fantasies you can do it all; even what we tried to do and couldn't."

"We *could* have! We just didn't give it enough time."

"Maybe," she said. "Probably. But the time is all gone, Jackie."

"Fair enough," he said. "But I'll tell you this—if I ever meet another girl like you, maybe I *will* get married."

"And maybe pigs *will* fly," she said. "Either way, right now you better get me a cab before this slope gets slippery."

Munich, 1973

Nuffing's What it Seems

The Nazi menace had never been so extreme and immediate as it was on the night of May 14th, 1973, at two o'clock in the morning, which was about forty years too late for any historian to make note of it.

That's when the man called Action roared into Jackie Barron's life on a dark street in Munich. Johnny Action was headed towards him at 60 miles per hour on a Harley-Davidson motorcycle, standing up on the pegs, firing an antique German Luger and singing *Rule, Britannia.*

It was scary, but not nearly so scary as the street had been a minute earlier. The shots from the Luger interrupted three post-adolescent neo-Nazis who had followed Jackie from a bar into the street at closing time. They had just begun creating an alternate version of World War II in which Jackie, representing America, was to be severely beaten.

The appearance of a madman singing and firing a gun changed the logistics of battle, and the amateur Storm Troopers retreated instantly.

Johnny Action hit the brakes, went into a hook-slide and came to a dramatic halt.

"It's about goddamn time you got here," Jackie said, checking his body-parts to see that he hadn't absorbed any stray bullets. "It was really you they wanted to beat up. We're in Germany, for chrissake; not everybody thinks it's funny when you stand up on top of a table and sing *Tomorrow Belongs to Me* with a comb stuck under your nose." He paused. "Why *did* you come back?"

"Well, you had the look of a man who was going to stay till closing time," Johnny Action said, "and that can get dodgy around here. I took care of a little business and dropped back by just in case."

"Good thinking. Now let's get out of here before the *polizei* bust you for trying to shoot people."

Johnny Action aimed the gun at Jackie and then turned the barrel toward his own temple and fired another shot.

"Not to worry," he said. "I designed this baby so's it doesn't even shoot blanks. Makes a beautiful noise, though, don't it?"

And so a friendship began.

The two had been introduced earlier in the week on the set of *The Hounds of Hell*, an eight-hour American television film based on a best-selling novel about the Third Reich. Jackie, as the Indie Broadcasting Network publicist for the miniseries, was there to write a behind-the-scenes book about the filming. The man called "Action" was in the Props Department, although, if described that way, he would automatically file a correction: "I'm not *in* the fookin Props Department. I *am* the fookin Props Department."

Jackie had heard tales of the Magnificent Madman. Everyone who had worked on locations with English crews seemed to know Johnny Action. Professionally, his specialty was finding props that were impossible to find—a 1943 Philco radio in contemporary Budapest; a Zippo lighter with the Marine Corps insignia in Romania; a hula-hoop in southern Italy—and he found them for every major movie that would put up with his personal habits. He was a lifelong Londoner, but he had developed a network of sources which included thrift shops, sidewalk-hustlers and trustworthy forgers all over Europe.

His other specialty was a high-risk exuberance for life on the edge; he was fond of saying *The 70s won't last forever; why should I?*

Jackie grew accustomed to seeing Action at the bar in the crew's hotel after the day's filming, sometimes moving on to a beer garden where he could agitate the natives. Most nights the restless Cockney would disappear by himself at closing time, heading off to meet with a band of shady characters in some after-hours joint that only he knew about, or to the bed of yet another local girl (or two). He was what every grip, gaffer and best-boy on the crew wanted to be.

Jackie also quickly discovered that Hollywood actors accustomed to starring roles were thrilled to be supporting players in a night of debauchery with the living legend. When they got home they would dine out on the sordid details for months.

The morning after the adventure in Munich, Jackie told the story to everyone on the set, and they had no trouble believing it. They all listened politely but mostly they were just waiting for him to finish so they could top his Johnny Action story with their own. Action, all agreed, was a pisser.

Some people knew his real name was John William Acton. Once he might even have been called that; now only the taxman ever thought of him that way. His friends just called him Action.

He stood an unimposing 5'9" with a body made up entirely of wire and knots. He was probably somewhere in his forties: no one knew exactly. He seemed to have more teeth than other people, and the grin—on loan from a wolf—made him ageless. The bags under his eyes, and the lines that his gray-flecked beard didn't hide, made him ancient.

His accent came and went like the coins that danced between his fingers when he did magic tricks. Sometimes his words were so drenched in the sound of Bow Bells and the pushcart peddlers of London's East End that it seemed he might choke on the aitches he was swallowing when he said 'e's got 'is 'eart set on goin' 'ome. When talking to the Americans in the production unit his speech could become so picturesque as to be near indecipherable: somefink is better than nuffink or arf a tick there, cocko; we've gah a hard day's graft ahead.

"I sound like fookin Gielgud if I want to," he would explain when challenged. "It's all a question of wha' I'm saying to *whom* and how the fook I'm feelin' at the moment." By the time Jackie Barron arrived in Munich, Johnny Action had half the Yanks in the unit learning rhyming slang. Like adding garlic to a stew, he always seemed to know when enough was enough. The Americans loved it while the rest of the Brits on the crew shook their heads and applauded his brass.

Off the set, he was the kind of good company Jackie had been told he would be—high-energy and fearless, considering no man a stranger, at ease on every social level—and embracing every controlled substance anybody had ever heard of. (He had, after all, first earned his nickname while slam-banging around the world as a roadie with a rock 'n' roll band in the 60s.) On the set he got the job done—drunk or sober, straight or stoned—like no one else alive.

"If you need sumfin for a scene and it exists, you'll have it before we wrap this afternoon," he would say. "If it don't exist you'll have to wait 'til tomorrow mornin'."

Jackie got a look at this expertise, which extended beyond the film's specific needs, when Action—with a lion tamer's cool-headed finesse—put himself into the middle of the daily disputes with Fran Doloman. She was the aging and arrogant American actress playing the wife of Joseph Goebbels, and over the years she had descended from movie star to sporadically-employed Special Guest Star on TV. The descent had left her notoriously insecure, bitter and mean. It also made her determined to assure everyone else's misery.

One day Jackie noticed Action consulting quietly with the producer and the wardrobe mistress, both of whom seemed puzzled but agreeable. Action then solemnly presented the star with a jeweled necklace while the company looked on.

"It's not my job, but I've been doin' a little searchin' around while we've been here," he said, "and I've found something I think you should wear in the ball-scene. The rest of the world won't know, but you'll know. This necklace belonged to Marlene Dietrich; she wore it in *The Blue Angel*. You can see it in this still from the movie. It wasn't easy to come by, but it's worth it—this necklace graced the neck of a great star of that time, and it belongs around the neck of a great fookin star of our time."

Fran Doloman was deeply, dramatically moved. She threw her arms around him and she wept. "You belong to an age of grace I thought was dead," she said. "God bless you!" For the remaining three days of her stay she was a gracious star in the grand manner.

When she left, the necklace left with her.

"Jesus," Jackie said when he heard this. "Dietrich's necklace? That was a *very* expensive gesture."

"All in the job," the props-master said. "Besides which, the photo only cost me a pound and the flea-market guy who copied the necklace owed me a favor. Worked, di'n it?"

Jackie had a new hero. "Action," he said, "you are so full of shit you gurgle. My kinda guy."

Johnny Action bowed and accepted the compliment graciously. "That's me, mate. If you can't dazzle 'em with brilliance, blind 'em with bullshit."

Jackie stayed in Europe with the film unit for ten weeks, and the friendship that blossomed on a Munich street developed into a lot of world-class but mercifully blanked-out drinking sessions. The vaudeville-sound of their combined first-names—suggesting something like *"Jackie & Johnny; Songs & Funny Stories"*—was annoying, so the man called Action eliminated it. For years Jackie had worn a weather-beaten leather hat with a feather in the band, and Johnny Action decided Jackie was Yankee Doodle. He called him Doodle for the rest of the shoot.

When European filming wrapped on *The Hounds of Hell* Jackie flew home to New York, staying in touch with Johnny Action only through the *give him my bests* carried between them by mutual friends.

In his behind-the-scenes book about the mini-series Jackie devoted a whole chapter to the skills and the charisma of Johnny Action, who just needed a few extra hours if you wanted the impossible, and he sent a copy to his friend. The people on a film crew were non-people to show-biz journalists, so he knew the movie veteran would be delighted to see his name in print for the first time.

Johnny Action had never been one for correspondence, but he sat down and wrote an enthusiastic letter of thanks, including his gratitude that Jackie had chosen not to write about some of the nights in Munich that would have made great but better-left-untold stories. Doodle, he wrote, had treated him like a pro, and it felt good. Being picturesque all the time could be tiring.

"I read the part about myself to the wife," the letter said, "and then I read it on the phone to my mum. She said that was very nice; did being in a book pay as well as being in a movie?"

Their next meeting was two years later, in Chamonix. (Action pronounced it Shamo-*NIX*, and soon everybody else did, too.)

Jackie had been on the location for three days when he was offered an unwelcome opportunity to repay the Munich favor by saving Action's ass.

The incident involved Vincent Miccelli, the hard-drinking and violently jealous star of the movie. He was convinced that someone in the company was having an affair with his girlfriend, and his suspicions were directed mostly at Johnny Action.

His suspicions were well placed, which is why Action knocked on Jackie's door at six a.m. on a Sunday morning.

"Vinnie's gone fookin looney-tunes," he said. "He's floatin in Johnnie Walker Black and some kinda Cambodian shit, and he swears he's gonna kill Jeannie and whoever she's been fucking."

"Oh, God. Where is he now?"

"Jeannie smashed the telephone over his head. It's all right; he's not dead or anything. But he'll not be best pleased when he comes to."

"And what about her?"

"She's all right. She's hiding in my room, but that's the first place he'll look. So I thought we could put her in here with you."

"Oh, that's *good* thinking," Jackie said. "If he finds her in here *I'm* the dead man. Is this me repaying you for Munich?"

"Not to worry. He'll never look for her in your room. He thinks you're a poof."

"Vincent Miccelli thinks I'm gay? Why on earth would he think that?"

"Well ... because that's what I told him. A little lie for your own protection, in case something like this should ever happen. I'm always watching out for you, mate."

As usual, Action's foresight was accurate. Jeannie slept on the couch in Jackie's room while the actor stormed through the hotel in an anguished search without ever knocking on Jackie's door. The next morning, when

Miccelli was full of sobs and apologies, Jeannie forgave him and took him back.

"I forget, Action," Jackie said. "Have I mentioned lately that you're fucking crazy? Why do you do this stuff? Your wife is terrific. I met her when we were in Munich, remember? She's an understanding woman, but if some jealous husband doesn't kill you eventually, she will."

"Never happen, Doodle. It's not like I really *cheat* on her. I'm geographically monogamous. I may not always be the dream husband, even when I'm at home, but there's no other birds in my life when I'm with Molly. None. But when I'm working on location somewhere ... well, that's never-never land. Molly doesn't ask. That's why we'll always last. She doesn't ask, and I don't lie. Very often."

Vincent Miccelli and Jeannie Burns left the following week, and the whole thing became just one more great story that Jackie knew he would never pass around.

When Jackie arrived in Zagreb on a JAT flight from New York in 1981, that all seemed like another lifetime, but it was a lifetime he wouldn't have missed. He was there for yet another World War II drama, as was Johnny Action, and Jackie looked forward to again watching him make props appear from unlikely places and women disappear from anything resembling sanity. They had been out of touch for a long time, and Jackie looked forward to the reunion.

After checking in at the Intercontinental Hotel he went directly to the location, an old Army base that had been turned into a 1943 German training ground. Johnny Action was there, looking much the same except for a little more gray in his beard and a little more belly straining against his belt. They went through the ritual greetings—*How you doin'?—Hangin' out and hangin' on, mate; hangin' out and hangin' on. You?—Too soon to tell, pardner; too soon to tell*—and agreed to meet for a drink at day's end.

Watching a scene being set up, Jackie realized there were more changes in Action than he had first noticed. The energy was still there in the face but it seemed to lag in the body. Action had been known to weave and stumble a bit at four in the morning, but it was not something he had ever allowed to happen on the set. And—again, something not alien to the witching hours but unheard-of during the day—now he occasionally tripped over a word, or slurred just the slightest bit. His energy was high and his wit had the same gravely edges, but a lot of things seemed to have changed in the six years since Chamonix.

Jackie knew the unit production manager from other shoots, and he carefully brought up the subject of Johnny Action. He didn't like what he heard. Maybe the night was finally demanding a ransom that even the legend couldn't cover.

A few hours later the two friends were at the bar—Action choosing to stand; Jackie seated on a stool—at the Interconti, lifting a drink to the old days—except that Jackie's hand was now wrapped around a Yugoslavian sparkling water called *Zoza Loza*.

"You want to explain that, mate?" Action said, his inquisitive grin as vaguely satanic as ever. "Yankee Doodle not drinkin'? That's not dandy. You on probation for something? Can't be an ulcer because a serious geezer like you isn't going to let that stop him. What kinda weird tale you gonna weave for me?"

"No weaving, Action,' Jackie said. "No wobbling, either. I just couldn't do it anymore."

Johnny Action took a long drink from his own glass. He didn't say anything, just arched his eyebrows toward the ceiling, tilted his head back and to the left, and locked eyes with his friend. He was waiting for Jackie's follow-up.

"Don't get nervous," Jackie said. "I got sober; I didn't get holy. I'll even buy the next round. Your bartender was hiding whatever he was mixing for you back there, so it must be a killer."

"It's called Long Island Iced Tea. Vodka, tequila, rum and gin. Equal parts. Crushed ice. One splash of Coca-Cola and one brisk shake. Remember Vinnie Miccelli?"

"Do I remember Vinnie Miccelli? You mean the charming and boyish actor you set up to break my neck? I'm not real sure what that has to do with anything, but—you bet your ass I remember him. The production company wasn't too happy about paying for the elevator he totaled; I was just grateful it wasn't my back."

"You see what a favor I did you by making him think you were a poofster? Probably saved your life. Anyway, I worked with him again after that and we became good mates. He taught the drink to me and I taught it to this bartender. You really not drinkin' at all?"

Jackie shook his head and shrugged. "Not today. Or yesterday. I'll worry about tomorrow tomorrow." Jackie grinned and dropped his voice to a solemn register. "One day at a time, Action. One fookin day at a time."

There was something victorious in Johnny Action's subdued yelp. "I knew it! You're Alcoholics bloody Anonymous!"

"Who, me? I'm just Jackie bloody Inscrutable. I don't worry about being anonymous. I was anonymous like the Statue of Liberty when I was drinking. I'm not going to be ashamed of getting sober."

"Yeah, yeah. You're AA. Let's go over to the little bar on the other side of the room; there's never anybody there."

When they were by themselves, Action said softly: "All right; here's the thing, mate. If even two AA people get together, that's a *meeting*, in' that right? And everything that's said in a meeting is confidential. Can't be discussed with anybody else, in' *that* right?"

"Ah, you movie people know everything," Jackie said.

"Fuck 'movie-people,' Doodle. I know the hard way. You remember I told you I had a rule about not fookin' around at home? Well ... these last few years that wasn't workin' so good. I didn't always make it home. Finally Molly got a call one day from a bird I was workin' with at Pinewood. She was screamin' at Molly. *Woman*, she says, *your husband is cheatin' on us*! That kinda tore it. They talked and Molly heard all the things she knew but didn't want to really *know*. When I got home she wasn't there. And she never came back."

Jackie held up a cautionary hand. "Action," he said, "*Your Husband is Cheating On Us* is an old blues song. Can we get some reality here?"

"Oh, don't get so fookin *particular*! All right; maybe I made that part up. Whatever it was she said, it did the job.

When we finally sat down to talk, Molly said she was tired of bein' deaf, stupid and blind and bein' the punchline to Johnny Action stories. Tired of bein' The Faithful Little Woman while The

Mis-*chie*-vious Rascal went out playin'. She was tired of a lot of stuff. Tough to argue with."

Jackie didn't have a crisp answer. "I'm sorry to hear that, Johnny. You guys were good together."

"Yeah, that's what you always said. And you were right. When she went, the good times went with her, and I was havin' whole days that I couldn't remember. And more that I didn't want to remember. And I've been AA for thirteen months and eight days." John William Acton said it all in one breath. Then he took a deep one.

So did Jackie Barron. "And ... that glass in your hand?" he finally said.

"There's a reason you couldn't see the bartender mix it. I tip him fifteen hundred dinars a week, which is serious money in Zagreb. For that kind of cash he makes me a genuine authentic mind-bender drink with no alcohol in it and nobody's the wiser. It's the show-business, Doodle," he said, tapping the side of his nose. "Nuffing's what it seems."

"All right. Okay. Help me out here. I talked to some of the guys on the set, and they're worried about you. You show up most mornings hobbling around like Quasimodo. You're pushing the envelope too hard at night, even for you, and they're afraid to talk to you about it."

"Good. They're supposed to be. Tell me this: anybody say I'm not doin' the job?"

"No. Nobody's saying that. But I'll also tell you this—the production manager told me flat-out: if anybody else showed up as spaced-out as you are now they'd be on the next plane back to London. You're still the best, Action, but nobody remembers ever seeing you this wasted. Now you tell me you've been sober for a year —"

"Thirteen months and eight days."

"All right; sober for thirteen months and eight days but you don't want anybody to know it. If you're not drinking, what kinda shit *are* you into?"

Johnny Action waited another moment before making the commitment.

"As long as there's nobody here but us two old drunks," he said, "it's an AA meeting. And that makes you the same as a priest, right? You're not allowed to tell anybody anything."

"Jesus Christ, Action, I'm not sure the Supreme Court would agree with you on that. But I do. So just get on with it. Doesn't matter anyway, *all* publicists swear an oath to secrecy. I'd get boils on my tongue if I gossiped."

"You've got a smart mouth on you, Doodle. Always had a smart mouth on you." Johnny Action finished off his *faux* cocktail and chewed a sliver of ice. "I've got Parkinson's fookin Disease, mate. Ain't that a bitch? Usually doesn't come out before sixty, and I'm not much past fifty. Always aheada me time."

That bomb excavated a whole new cavern of silence. Johnny Action finally broke it.

"You gonna ask me why I pretend I'm still strung out on the good times? Or have you already figured it out?"

"You tell me."

Action shrugged. "It's simple, mate. They're not gonna hire somebody with Parkinson's for the bloody crew; not even me. You say the word *Parkinson's* and they imagine some poor sod who shakes and jerks and scares the horses in the street. But if I show up with a hangover that's eatin' me alive—and still get everything where it has to be ten minutes before it has to be there—doesn't matter if I look like Keith Richards with bad lighting. I don't get replaced. I get *respect*. I get respect because even the bosses wish *they* could do it, and when they go home they brag about how they worked with this fantastic guy called Johnny Action who looks like Caligula's wet-nurse but gets it *done*, mate; he gets it bloody *done*.

"The lads on the crew wonder where I go at night? Well, how about this: if it's been a hard day—and on this fookin picture they all are—I go to bed hurtin' in places other people don't even have."

Action stopped abruptly and waved a dismissive hand in front of his face, sweeping his own words away. "Self-pity don't make for good show-biz, mate, so just forget I said that."

The look of cynical amusement that Jackie remembered from the old days reappeared magically when the waitress checked to see if they wanted another round. "Why not," Johnny Action said. "The 80s won't last forever, either. Just make sure Zivko knows it's for me."

When she was gone he said "Where was I? Oh, yeah. I stand up all the time because getting out of a chair is hard and clumsy and it hurts. I hang out with some Saudi tourists at the hotel because they're pharmacists and their license is good here. They get me amphetamines legally.

My doctors wouldn't approve because the speed'll probably kill me before the Parkinson's does, but it eases some things. And I never said I wanted to live forever, now did I?"

Johnny Action lit a cigarette—proving that he didn't want to live forever—and clamped it between his front teeth, grinning the grin that was almost as famous as his exploits. He took a deep drag, held the cigarette at the base of his first two fingers, took it out of his mouth and talked through the smoke as he exhaled.

"Just look at me," he said, spreading his arms expansively. "Kids use these drugs to go crazy in nightclubs and I'm a middle-aged man using them to look normal. And get this: *After* I stopped drinking, *then* I read that alcohol might reduce the risk of Parkinson's! My usual timing.

"You gotta love it, Doodle: I can keep workin' as long as they think I stumble and slur because I'm burnin' my rocket at both ends. That's colorful, mate, and in this b'iness you get away with murder if you're *colorful.*"

Johnny Action shook his head and looked off into the distance, the smile of the wolf still in place and the cigarette back between his teeth.

"Funny old world, innit?"

New York, 2010

As Time Went By

When former Corporal Darby James reappeared, it came as a major shock to Jackie Barron.

"Darby, you are maybe the last person on earth I would ever have expected to show up at my door. How'd you find me?"

"You forget fast," Darby said. "Where you're living now is where you were living forty-some years ago, which was the last time I saw you. You told me then you'd probably die in this apartment. I didn't figure you'd be dead yet."

They had been friends in the Army—which was fifty years ago for Jackie; Darby kept on re-enlisting for another twenty-seven years. They remained friends for a long time after Jackie got out, even driving through a blizzard to Miami together to celebrate the end of his two years in the Army. Over the years they had lost touch, until Darby showed up unannounced.

"So—where've you been for forty years?"

Darby shrugged. "Around. Just not around New York. I came up on a little... business... so I figured I'd drop by." Darby laughed. "I didn't call first 'cause I thought your phone might be tapped."

Jackie remembered that his friend had planted a small but promising marijuana field in Florida when he retired.

"You know people whose phones are tapped? I'm impressed. Never dreamed you'd be such a big-time operator in boojum-business. You've come a long way from the Fort Dix Motor Pool."

Darby cackled and said, "Now, *that's* why I wanted to see you again. You're probably the only living person besides me who would call marijuana *boo*. We're the last of a dying breed, Jackie."

"I'm sure that's true. The difference is, I haven't smoked a joint in at least thirty years."

"Well, I don't burn up my inventory the way I used to, either. I remember you told me once you'd quit drinking, too. How long you been sober?"

"All day," Jackie said. "The guy who's been sober longest is whoever got up first this morning. I've been getting up sober for 34 years."

"Well, I never would've seen that coming. What about Cassie Sullivan? You two used to tie on some beauties together."

"Well, Cassie was one of those oddities that alcoholics never understand: a social drinker. After we broke up—for the third or fourth time —"

"I think you were on your third the last time we talked."

"Point is, she quit drinking about the same time she quit me. Said she wasn't sure which was going to kill her first."

"That's too bad. I liked her."

"So did I. So did everybody. After that last breakup she married an old high school boyfriend and moved west. I haven't seen her for fifteen years or so, but we exchange birthday cards."

"How old is she now?"

"I never asked, Darby. But she couldn't have her heart surgery until her Medicare kicked in a couple of years ago."

"How'd that work out? She okay?"

"Yeah; she's fine."

"And you? How's your health, old man?"

"Oh... a little prostate cancer radiation; a little lung surgery. The usual stuff."

"I like your attitude," Darby said, looking around the room. "You're still not married, right? With all these goddamn books you wouldn't have room for a woman."

"Actually, I gave it a try. I wasn't good at it. What about you?"

"Naw. I've heard it can be a good thing, but... I never could see much point to it. You still living here alone?"

"Yup. I've been happily keeping company with the same woman for twenty-two years—my previous record was two. We keep it real by not marrying or living together."

"Now, that I can understand. I just never met a *woman* who could."

"Never too late, Darby. Seems to me like you always had a woman in your life anyway."

"Yeah, well. Speaking of which... there's something I never told you. Remember when you broke up with Crazy Debbie?"

"I didn't 'break up with her.' I fled from her."

"Well... she fled to me. I didn't think you'd mind. We had some good weeks—but then she stuck her head in the oven—again. She wound up in Bellevue—again—and I went home to Florida, which put us both where we belonged. Is she in or out these days?"

"I have no idea," Jackie said. "I picked her up from Bellevue a couple of times in the 80s, but no more."

"Let's see... what else do I want to know? What about that amyl nitrate Sunday-Popper-Society you and your Hollywood bunch had in the 60s? They all dead or in jail?"

"Absolutely not. Mickey works on a movie or two every year and lives good. Marvin went into rehab for pills and then became an agent. Alex Venture's series finally got cancelled but he hasn't been out of work since."

"I went with you that one Sunday but I never met that actress who lived there," Darby said.

"That's no surprise. She was usually awake by 2:30 in the afternoon, but sometimes she went over schedule. She also tried suicide a few years later. Unfortunately she was better at it than Debbie was."

There was a moment of respectful silence before Darby said, "Jackie, the dopers who buy from me aren't nearly as interesting as the people you used to get high with."

"That's because we were just chippying around; we weren't really dopers."

"There you go again," Darby said. "I don't think anybody's called 'casual use' *chippying around* for about forty years."

"Well, about forty years ago was when we were doing it. Sometimes it's good to stay an amateur."

"Something must be working for you—you're still here. How old are *you* now?"

"Ahh... the immortal Gertrude Stein once said, *We are always the same age inside.* I think she was right," Jackie said. "And that makes me thirty."

Darby James studied him for a moment before saying, sadly, "Well... you don't look it."

New York, 1991

Dancing in the Dark

It was usually not until after his third drink in the backroom of the Broadcast Grill that Jackie Barron introduced the subject of Otto Winkler. This was generally a signal for those who knew him best to remember someplace they had to be.

On a good night there would be a few at the table who would take the hint and answer "No" when he asked "Can you tell me who Otto Winkler was?" That was all it took. The floodgates opened.

"You don't know who Otto Winkler was," he would say. "You're sitting in a bar full of publicists and other showbiz detritus and you don't respond with sorrow and despair at the name of Otto Winkler. What a world!"

"I plead guilty," said Randy Gerard, who was joining the after-work conclave for the first time. "I don't know who Otto Winkler was. What... he founded the network? He had a sitcom in the 50s? He used to be the bartender here?"

Before Jackie could respond he was interrupted by two of his friends who were hastily dropping dollar-bills on the table and excusing themselves. Two remained—Drew Lawrence, who knew what was coming but was still two drinks shy of going home, and Randy Gerard, who was so young he was delighted just to be included.

Ticking the count on one finger at a time, Jackie said: "The answer is no, no, no and *NO*!" Don't make guesses. The name sounds funny—it *is* funny—but the man deserves respect. You know why you never heard of him?

I'll tell you why you never heard of him. You never heard of him because he was *me*. And Drew. And, if you stick in here long enough—*you*.

"You never heard of him because he was a publicist. Not like the glamorous lady-publicists who get their own names in the columns these days. Otto Winkler was a working-class, union-brother, invisible-man-martyr whose death made the front pages... but his *name* didn't show up until page thirty. Below the fold"

So began Jackie's rant about the Hollywood publicist who had gone on a War Bond tour with Carole Lombard in 1942. She had overruled Otto's plea that they continue travelling by train and insisted that they charter a plane home. The airplane she insisted they take crashed against a mountain and killed everybody on board.

"That's the nutshell, my very young friend," Jackie said after assaulting Randy Gerard with the story. "You weren't born then, but I'll bet you know who Carole Lombard was, and I'll bet you know how she died. But *you*—a working publicist—you never heard of Otto Winkler. Well, he died in the seat next to her because *he* was a working publicist and that was his job. Outside of his immediate family I'm sure nobody noticed."

"Uh... I don't get it," Randy said. "Was he a friend of yours?"

"Oh for chrissake," Jackie said, "I was seven years old and running around barefoot in Tennessee when he died. He's a *symbol*, Randy; he's a *symbol*!"

Drew Lawrence leaned over the table and gripped Jackie's arm.

"Indoor voice, Jackie," he said. "Indoor voice. If you get too excited the lad won't understand a word you're saying."

Joanie, the waitress who covered the room where the group always sat, stopped by the table. She looked at Drew and asked: "Otto Winkler time?"

Drew just nodded and drew a circle with his finger, ordering another round for everyone.

"I'm not excited," Jackie said, sweeping the accusation away with his hand. "I'm just trying to make a very important point about our lives.

"The *point* is that Carole Lombard's death is famous because she was. Otto Winkler died *with* her, but he wasn't famous... so his death isn't either. That's our life, youngblood; get used to it. You walk off the set and everyone in the crowd waiting out there is openly disgusted with you for not *being* anyone. Half the stars you work with will refer to you as *that network guy*. And you never get invited to any A-list parties. Ever."

Drew interrupted again. "A little perspective here, Jackie. There were sixteen other people on that flight. Can you name *them*?"

"That's a cheap shot," Jackie said. "You know I can't. Neither can anyone else who isn't a blood relation. But we're talking about the show-business here; those other people were civilians.

"It's not just us," he went on. "There's a whole underbelly world of people who are barely even remembered when they're in the room. You remember Arthur Marx? No, right? But he understood. He used to say 'If I go down in a plane-crash the headline will say SON

OF GROUCHO DIES. That's because his father was famous. And Arthur Marx was even lower than a publicist in the Hollywood pecking order. He was a *writer*!"

"I don't know if I'd really want to be famous," Randy said. "I like being behind-the-scenes. I read about stars complaining all the time that people bother them on the streets and in restaurants, always telling them how great they are. They just wish people would leave them alone."

"Yeah, well, I hope they do. Let the people come and ask for *my* autograph," Jackie said. "You can bet your ass *I'll* be gracious about it."

Drew played devil's advocate: "If you hate it so much, why don't you quit and become a star yourself?"

"You know who likes a smartass, Drew? Nobody, that's who. And quitting wouldn't make any difference. I've got terminal obscurity in my veins. You know what my job was before I came to the network? I was a nationally syndicated newspaper columnist. Only my byline said: *by Robert J. Richards*. Never *by Jackie Barron.* Because Robert J. Richards could barely write his name but the sonofabitch owned the damn syndicate and he wanted people to *think* he was a writer.

"It gets worse. I also wrote a daily column—one that didn't get his byline. It was a Letters column about television and the byline was exclusively mine. But not *Jackie Barron.* I was *The Answer Man.*

"Warhol told a cruel lie when he promised everybody that fifteen minutes. I haven't had mine, and I'm damned if I can see it coming up anytime soon. Or late. Can you?"

Drew Lawrence, feeling the effect of the last few drinks himself, responded with profundities: "Well, fame is fleeting, Jackie. Fame... is a cruel mistress. Fame ain't what it used to be and it never was."

Even drunk, Jackie was too good a friend to call Drew on his non-sequiturs.

"You want to hear one more?" he said. "I'll tell you one more publicist story, and it's a doozie.

"You know who wrote *Alone Together* and *By Myself* and *That's Entertainment?* I'll tell you who wrote the words for those songs. A *publicist* wrote those words. That's right. A publicist. Do you know his name? Oh, put your hand down, Drew; you know because I already told you."

"No offense," Randy said, "But I think you're wrong. I'm pretty sure those are all Dietz and Schwartz songs."

"*Yes!* Yes, indeed; give that bright young man half-a-point for knowing everything but the point of the story.

"Here is the point of the story," Jackie continued. "You know what Howard Dietz's real job was? *Howard Dietz was a publicist*! Just like Otto Winkler—except that Dietz was a boss. He worked for MGM, and he also wrote all those 'Goldwynisms' like 'A verbal contract isn't worth the paper it's written on,' or: 'We've all passed a lot of water since then.'

"So, yeah; Howard Dietz *is* famous—but as a *songwriter*; not as one of the greatest publicists who ever lived. And I'll tell you one more secret. He agreed with me. He even hid our lives in one of his songs.

"He called it *Dancing in the Dark*."

Jackie looked around proudly. Nobody responded to this less-than-stunning revelation.

"Don't you see? It's a code. That's what *we* do. We shine the brightest lights in the world on other people... and *we* just keep dancing in the dark. Unseen. Dancing as fast as we can. Stumbling over our own feet. Tap-dancing without making a sound. Singing praises..."

Drew Lawrence got up from the table and walked around to Jackie's side, putting a hand on his friend's shoulder.

"You're right, Jackie. When you're right you're right. Now let's share a cab before you stand up on the table and start shouting."

Jackie Barron knew when the time had come. He threw a twenty on the table and stood up, ready to be delivered to a taxi.

"No," he said, "not shouting. Dancing. I'll just keep dancing. Nobody'll notice anyway."

Made in the USA
Lexington, KY
02 October 2013